CH01020341

The Other Side (

You never know what's on the other side of the door until you open it. It might be pleasant, it may be a shock, but one thing is for sure – it will be a surprise. Turn the handle and step inside to discover the mysteries and revelations that lie within.

This book exists thanks to Lou. He encouraged me to write, read draughts and made suggestions, but most importantly - he makes me feel I can fly.

Front & back covers: paintings by Lou Pizzi
© Lou Pizzi 2008

Paperback book ISBN: 978-1-291-99025-6
eBook ISBN: 978-1-291-40292-6

Stories

Stargazing

It was the middle of winter and freezing cold, but a crisp evening with a clear sky. That was why there were so many stars and the reason I went outside to stand gazing up at them.

It had been one of those days when everything went wrong; the computer programme I was working on refused to cooperate and I had only managed to get it to do what it was told around 8.00 pm.

By that point I had gone past being hungry, so decided to have a hot shower and get into my pyjamas, then sit in front of the fire watching a DVD, with a hot cup of tea and some toast.

I had got as far as having the shower, but having a roof window in the bathroom I had noticed the stellar spectacle in the sky, so quickly donning cotton pyjamas and a dressing gown, and slipping my feet into "slip on" slippers, I dashed outside to stargaze. I had only intended going out for a few minutes but...............

Next thing I knew was - the front door closed and locked.

At first I couldn't believe it. I had been alone in the house and kept the door locked all day – so I was sure of that. I had been working on the programme for three days non-stop and I hadn't opened it in that time. Standing outside I had only taken one step outside the door, so there was not enough space for anyone to have passed me unnoticed.

I tried the door, but sure enough it was locked. Locking it was not easy; it was one of those ones where you had to pull the handle up before the key would turn, and that meant someone had to do it - it definitely could not happen alone.

Now I was worried. There was someone in the house!

I thought about my options, but - I lived in the country, with my nearest neighbour about two miles away down a steep road, and I was wearing thin, short pyjamas and partially open slippers. There was so much ice you slipped just looking at it and the temperature was minus something or other.

Could I make it with these slippers and the icy road to the farmhouse? Unlikely, but if there was someone in my house, staying here was not a good option either as they were probably dangerous.

That thought made me take a step back and I slipped and fell.

As I sprawled there stunned, not just at the fall, but at everything that was happening, the lock turned and the door opened again.

Shivering from cold I surveyed my options again, and getting inside to try and get the car keys and my phone, and maybe a pair of shoes, was undoubtedly the best thing.

Heart pounding I stepped inside gingerly and looked round. I couldn't see anyone, but as I had not switched on the light earlier so as not to disturb my view of the stars, it was hard to tell.

If I could make no sound and move about in the dark, I reasoned, I would have the advantage as I knew the house better, so I took a couple more steps.

In the silence, the door closing and key being turned seemed to sound like a death knell and I whirled round, straining my eyes, but still no one was visible.

It was at this point I became really frightened. The intruder was within touching distance of me, and could do whatever they liked to me as I had nothing to defend myself with.

I tried asking what they wanted in an alarmingly wavy voice, but got no answer. That lack of reply was the worst thing they could have done, and was more frightening than anything they could have said.

I tried suggesting if they told me what they wanted maybe I could help, hardly an original idea, but by then my logic process had stayed outside, frozen solid. Again no answer.

Standing there in the hall I watched the door into the kitchen slowly close. Next was the door into the lounge, followed by the bathroom door and the other three visible doors, until only the study door stayed open.

My thoughts were telling me he wanted me to go into the study, but neither my voice nor my feet seemed to be working anymore, so I just stood there in silence until........... I felt a gentle push on my back. I was too frightened by this point to turn round, and was still processing everything when the push got a little firmer. I moved in little steps until I was standing in the study where, yet again, the door closed.

Was I alone in here or was he with me? The only blackout curtains in the house were doing their job too well, and it came to me that maybe these heavy curtains were the reason I was here. This was the darkest room in the whole house.

I wanted to think of a plan, but my mind was focused on panic instead of logic, and 'oh no' was the only thought that was clear.

I don't know how long I stood there and I don't know if I was alone or not. It is strange, I always thought you would feel another presence, sense it or just know it was there somehow, but that was not how it worked for me. Another strange thing was; at first I stood there shaking but after a while that stopped and I felt calmer – still afraid, but not so panicky.

Nothing happened for a while, and then the door opened and all the lights in the house went on at the same time. Every single one!

Having light gave me a bit more courage and I moved out of the study into the hall, and just as I was passing the phone - it rang.

I jumped three feet into the air and found I had spontaneously reached out to pick it up without thinking.

A dead sounding voice asked for Mr Brandon, and when I said that was me, the voice asked could I come to the hospital in Genoa. "Not easily as I am thousands of miles away in a different country," was my reply, so the disembodied voice said it had some sad news for me – my elder brother had just died.

It went on to explain, in bad English, that my brother was in that area on holiday, and he had had an accident in his car while driving through a tunnel. People had seen it happen and tried to help, but he lost consciousness before the ambulance got there. He was taken to the hospital where they did everything they could - but he had never regained consciousness and had not spoken.

I collapsed onto the floor and sat for a while.

Then I remembered my uninvited guest was still lurking in my home. I got the biggest kitchen knife I had, and set off to find whoever it was. I searched the house thoroughly, under the bed, behind doors, in wardrobes – everywhere, but there was no one there.

Should I call the police? And tell them what?

Nothing had happened except a few doors opening and closing. They might lock me up as a mental case, and right now I couldn't blame them.

I went into the kitchen and sat at the table unmoving until suddenly it came to me, and I had it all figured out.

The door closing when I was outside was him having an accident or perhaps going into the tunnel, my fall was when he hit whatever he hit, the door opening was people getting help, the door closing again is when he lost consciousness, standing in the study represents him in a coma in hospital and the door opening and the light on is when he died.

Somehow this explanation did little to comfort me and I wondered why it had happened to me and if it would happen again.

Still sitting stunned I heard the kettle switch off and smelt toast – but I had not put the kettle on and had not put bread into the toaster.

Cat Burglar

In a series of small villages where rich people went to pretend they were 'Lord of the Manor', a series of burglaries occurred. As these homes were full of treasures, the amount stolen was rather large and the influence the owners had was considerable. This put the police under a great deal of pressure to solve the case, but they had no idea who was doing it, and no leads whatsoever.

The first robbery took place at the home of Madeline, a minor film star, where three diamond necklaces, bracelets, rings and other valuable items of jewellery were stolen while she was at a film premiere. These items had been kept in the safe in her bedroom, and the house had a good alarm system, but it had not been set off. The front door was open, so presumably the burglars went in that way, and the safe had been opened; neither door was forced, making it look like an inside job. Madeline had not installed CCTV, as she wanted no record of her numerous male guests, although publicly she said it was because she spent all day being recorded and felt the need for some privacy.

At first the police had thought it probable she had done it herself for some reason, (they couldn't think of a viable one as she did not need the money, and selling the jewellery would have netted her more than the insurance value), but soon had to rule her out as a suspect, especially when the second robbery happened soon after. There was also the problem of her intellect, or rather lack of it, and no one on the force really believed she could have planned and carried out this daring robbery.

The second case concerned valuable statues which were stolen from James, a bestselling author. The statues were not large, and had mostly been kept in his lounge in a special cabinet which had an extra security device in place. Again the alarm had not been tripped, no locks forced and no one had been seen either going in or out of the place. James had been asleep upstairs and had heard nothing, but was understandably frightened at the thought that someone had been in his house while he slept. This fear was heightened by the fact that James was blind and naturally felt unable to defend himself against an intruder. His loss of sight had made spectacular headlines, partly because he was famous, and partly as he was a writer. At the time newspapers had speculated that he may have to stop writing, but James hired a good secretary and simply dictated to her, either in person, or using a Dictaphone.

Like Madeline, James had no CCTV, but unlike her, his reasons were valid – he couldn't see what it showed and so it seemed pointless.

The third theft was of paintings and happened in the home of Richard, (Rick), a famous pop star. These were true works of art and were his prize possessions, and included two Constables, a Turner, and no less than three Gainsborough's, to say nothing of his Monet, small Rembrandt and a few others. Unusually, these had been removed along with the frames, making them extremely difficult to take away unnoticed – yet that is what happened. Nobody saw anything, and the CCTV footage showed no one entering or leaving. It appeared the burglar had entered by an upstairs window which had been left open slightly. Richard proclaimed loudly that he liked fresh air and often left his bedroom window open. A third floor window, at the back of a house with a sophisticated alarm system and electric boundary fence, had seemed safe enough to leave slightly open while he gave a concert one hundred miles away. Again the truth was slightly different – he had smoked a few joints in bed that morning, and the woman he intended to bring home with him thought he had stopped that particular habit, so the open window was to let any remaining fumes out.

This type of entry ruled out Madeline, a sixty something actress, or so she claimed, (actually it was seventy one), as a woman her age could not have climbed up to the window - and marks on the roof showed a grappling hook had been used rather than a ladder. That involved quite a climbing feat, and needed a strong person to shinny that sort of distance up a rope. James too could not have done it; as such an enterprise requires a fit person with full sight.

By now the desperate police thought the security company was responsible, as it was obvious someone had blocked or changed the CCTV footage, as well as knowing the access codes, but as Madeline used a different company to the other two victims, this did seem to be clutching at straws a bit.

Then five more burglaries happened in the same area. Each one was carried out in a different way and varying items were stolen. The only thing each robbery had in common was knowledge of the house: disarming the security, entering and moving round the houses efficiently was not a problem for the thief, and only the extremely valuable items were removed.

The residents of this hamlet were questioned numerous times to try and find a link; did they all use the same cleaners? What caterers did they use? Who cleaned their pools? On and on it went, but every person who entered one or two homes, did not enter the others. The company who had a connection with the most burgled houses provided flower arrangements for five of them. This was a gay, reedy florist whose arms were so thin you wondered how he managed to hold a vase of flowers - they would not support him for climbing a rope.

Every celebrity insisted the only people who knew their houses well were the other celebrities, as they often had parties, each inviting the other. Not from neighbourly good-will, but so they would be invited in return, and because, "one never knew who one might meet that could further one's career".

The police were convinced it was one of the home owners, but which one eluded them. In total there were twenty-three houses; six people were too old, one had a broken leg and one was blind, leaving fifteen possible cat burglars.

One extremely fat man and two weak women were also ruled out, as cat burgling seemed beyond their physical capabilities. Twelve suspects, but none fitted for all crimes and most had an excellent alibi for at least one crime. Rick was on stage with 50,000 adoring fans watching, to say nothing of TV cameras filming him; Madeline was being televised at a film premier a long distance away, and on it went.

Maybe two of them were working together, so while one had an alibi the other could rob the homes, was another theory, but there remained the insurmountable problem of how they knew the security codes and safe combinations. Each person hated the other and would not have given the code or even used it while the other was in their house.

The streak of robberies stopped at eight homes, and after a while the police moved onto murder, drunk driving and other crimes. The policeman who had headed up the investigation was close to retirement, and would have preferred his record to show he had solved this case, so, when his junior sergeant said he would like to keep digging, the chief willingly gave his consent.

Time passed and Madeline starred in a hit film taking her where she had always wanted to be – into the real film star category. James, feeling insecure after his intruder experience, sold his house and moved to the south of France, where he wrote two more spy stories which both hit the bestseller list, and Rick had a number one song and number two album. The sergeant slogged on with his investigation, but made no progress; none of the stolen items turned up anywhere. The senior officer on the cat burglar case retired, and both the press and the public soon forgot about the series of famous robberies. Eventually even the sergeant gave up as a promotion and new-born twin daughters took his mind elsewhere.

The policemen who had dealt with the case were promoted, demoted and otherwise moved to different areas, therefore when one of the celebrities involved came onto their radar again there was no one left who personally remembered details about the case.

Madeline had a role in a Hollywood blockbuster where she had to play the police chief, so she approached her local barracks, asking if she could stay there for a few days to observe how things were done. The new young policemen were thrilled at having a film star in their barracks and agreed willingly.

When any of the policemen had a spare few minutes they all gravitated to her, whereupon she asked them about work, and in return for their information answered their questions about films, film stars and Hollywood.

One day a new recruit asked her about the film she was working on and she told him it was already a bestselling book by the famous author James Johns. Not being a book fan, the youngster had never heard of Johns, but one of the older men had, and inquired whether Johns hadn't lived locally in the past.

Madeline replied that he had, but explained how he had been worried after the robbery and had left. She went on to say his book about burglary was being made into a film and she was playing the police chief who investigated. She said it was all so very exciting as it was so similar to what had happened to her all those years ago.

One of the policemen present that day pricked his ears and went over to hear everything she said better. He was fascinated by crime, and his hobby was looking over unsolved crimes. The "China Cat" robberies had got his interest as few others had, mainly because there were never really any suspects.

He asked Madeline if this was the same case, and she said it was. He then asked why the name "China Cat", and was rewarded with the explanation that one of the precious statues stolen from James Johns had been a china cat, and as it was taken by a cat burglar the press had come up with that nick name. James used that title for his book, she went on, "isn't that a coincidence?"

The policeman wondered if it might be a bit more than that, and leaving work early he went straight to a book shop to buy the book.

He started it that night and read all through the night until he had finished. Next he went onto the internet and checked a few things - then he wrote a report which he handed to his boss the next day.

His boss read it and called him in.

"Constable, are you certain about all this?"

"Yes sir."

"And the doctor confirmed Johns got his sight back before he moved to live here?"

"Yes sir. No one checked beyond the fact he had lost sight in both eyes and the fact it came back was never brought up. His accident and subsequent blindness was in all the papers, and the possibility he would see again was never mentioned. It is all in the book, including how useful it was for people to think he was blind as they opened their safes in front of him and he memorised the codes. The same with the alarms - and when people found him wandering round their houses, instead of being angry, they felt sorry for him. The book came out the day after the statute of limitations ran out.

"I wonder what he did with the loot, sergeant."

"Well, sir, Madeline says they have reproductions in the film that are so good they look exactly like the real thing."

Last Minute Trip

Having just broken up with my girlfriend of seven years, I decided on the spur of the moment to take a week off work and go away somewhere.

I looked on the internet for package deal holidays leaving the next day, and booked the cheapest. It didn't matter to me where I went; in my current state of mind nowhere inspired me. All I wanted was to get away and be somewhere where there were no memories, I knew no one, and had no decisions to make – hence the package deal.

It turned out someplace I had never heard of in Spain called Guardamar was to be my "thinking and re-grouping" respite.

I threw a pair of jeans and a pair of trousers, a jumper and a shirt, a pair of shoes and a jacket into a case and closed it. After lunch, during a flash of common sense, I remembered essentials like socks, toothbrush and toothpaste, razor and shaving cream along with shower gel and shampoo and added them to my small bag.

That evening I sat in the dark with the phones all off and didn't answer the incessantly ringing door bell.

It had been that way since I walked into our bedroom yesterday and found my live-in girlfriend and my brother Nigel doing, "it isn't what it seems." It seemed they were having sex, but if that was not what was happening I really couldn't figure out what was. I could, however, figure out who was at the door and exactly what they would say should I open it - "I am sorry. I didn't mean to. I hope you can forgive me", then for good measure, "we need to put this behind us".

That last part was proving harder than it should be, and was the reason I knew what Nigel would say - it was what he had said nine years ago when I walked into my bedroom and found him having sex with my fiancée.

In the months following this first betrayal I had derived some small compensation when the errant fiancée discovered she was pregnant and, after heated paternity tests, it had turned out to be Nigel's. He had been forced to marry the promiscuous so and so and for years had been paying for school fees, riding lessons and massive orthodontist bills – to name but a few.

As the pain lessened we all started to meet at family gatherings, (for a while, with our parents help, I had made sure we went on different days), but things remained strained, not least as the loose woman, who was now my sister-in-law, had started coming on to me. By then my life was in such good shape I was able to say no and mean it, but I did enjoy thinking how she couldn't wait to deceive her husband, who was also my betraying brother.

At some point I must have fallen asleep, as I woke up on the couch with daylight visible through the curtains. In panic I looked at the time, but it was still early and I hadn't missed my flight.

A rushed breakfast, shower and shave, were followed by a hasty throwing on of clothes as I grabbed my small case and went to meet the horn blaring taxi waiting to take me to the airport.

I don't know if I slept on the journey or just sat in a daze, but remembering nothing of it I emerged from the airport into bright sunlight. It took a while for my eyes to adjust, but when they did I saw vast expanses of sandy looking terrain, palm trees, camels and men with long flowing robes.

The only Spanish town I knew was Barcelona, and this airport was further south, but even so this scene seemed more Arabic than Spanish. The only thought that stopped me from panicking was that it was impossible to get on the wrong flight as there were so many checks and controls to pass through before you were allowed on-board. Nevertheless, I got out my ticket, checked it did say 'Alicante', and having that confirmed I looked for the promised hotel transport.

There were no vehicles from 'Playa del Mar' in sight, so I set down my case to wait. A few minutes later I spotted one of the Arab looking men walking around and carrying a board with my name on it. I said with a foreign accent, "Yo soy el Señor Waterstone", but he just stared blankly. I hadn't thought my Spanish was bad enough to be incomprehensible but the man showed no sign of understanding. Trying a different tack, I pointed to the board and then to myself. That produced a relieved expression, a flurry of words spoken so quickly they were incomprehensible to me, and a sign to follow him as he snatched my bag.

Presumably the hotel had only one guest on that flight and I would get to travel to the hotel alone. Good! I didn't feel like making conversation with fellow tourists who, unlike me, would probably be bubbly and full of joy at being on holiday.

The "car" was a big, long white limo and when he opened the door for me I could see a bottle of champagne on ice. For the first time I became wary - two star hotels don't send massive limos like this. "Hotel Playa del Mar?" I queried. He nodded.

"Guardamar?" I tried too.

"Hotel Playa del mar, Guardamar" he confirmed, so I got in thinking two star hotels in Spain were not bad. Before driving off he uncorked the champagne and poured me a glass - so I rode through southern Spain in a chauffeur driven limo, sipping champagne and enjoying the view. I hadn't expected such luxurious treatment for the low price I had paid, but had no intention of protesting.

We seemed to be in an extensive desert with nothing except sand and an occasional palm tree. This wasn't what I had imagined, nor was it what I wanted – but that was my own fault for not looking closely at where the hotel I booked was. Somewhere in my mind I had envisioned wandering through streets flanked by historical buildings, sitting in old churches and relaxing in squares sipping something cold and alcoholic. From what I could see out the window I would have to spend the time in the hotel, as there seemed to be nothing nearby to do or see. Luckily, the weather was good and surely a hotel that sent a limo would have a pool, so a boozy day swimming and lazing around would have to do.

About an hour's driving took us into a town in the middle of the desert. There was no warning, just a sudden change of view out the side window, from everlasting sand to whitewashed walls. Perhaps sightseeing was on the cards after all.

The car stopped and the door was opened by a uniformed doorman, giving me my first glimpse of the hotel. It was amazing, and everything I saw gave the appearance of an expensive five star hotel. I went to the check in desk to fill out the necessary forms and found the hotel was extremely well organised. The manager greeted me by name, (in English), and without asking me to sign

14

anything, he picked up a key and suggested I follow him. He stopped in front of two large double doors and flung them open.

Wow! Majestic, regal, sumptuous – too expensive, was what went rapidly through my mind.

I turned and instantly the manager said, "You like it? It is the Sultan Suite, our best room."

Assuring him I did like it, I tried delicately to explain I was afraid it would cost more than I had intended spending. He reassured me it was what I had booked and paid for and there would be nothing else to pay.

Things were starting to feel out of sync, but I thanked him, and when he had left with the remark, "no tips allowed is hotel policy", I sat down on a sofa and took out my travel itinerary.

I wondered briefly if my conniving brother had found out about my trip and got me an upgrade; but he couldn't have known I was going away, never mind where. Something did not seem right. I had paid for two star accommodation, (and thought it cheap for the price), yet everything to do with this hotel yelled expensive luxury.

I searched all the documents, and read all the bits I had foolishly skipped when I had reserved the room, but there was only booking confirmation for 'a room and full board', no mention even of double or single, and I couldn't remember what I had put on the form. At least I had paid for it, and my papers confirmed 'paid in full', so they couldn't hound me for an exorbitant sum at a later date.

I unpacked my few belongings and while putting them away I realised I had brought neither pants nor deodorant.

There was just time before lunch to nip out and get them, and still thinking about the strange place that was not at all Spanish looking, I walked into a menswear shop and got pants. At the till the man said in English, "No, Sir", to my offer of Euro, "guests in the Sultan Suite do not pay for any essentials." While I was pondering this new twist he went on, "I took the liberty of adding two pairs of pyjamas, as you seem to have forgotten them too."

15

Before I had time to say anything he had excused himself and disappeared. As he did not appear again, and time was running out for getting to the chemist before it closed, I decided the best option was to take the package and talk to the hotel manager later. There was obviously some sort of arrangement or deal going on between the shop and the hotel.

With my mind occupied with my freebies, a doubt began to creep in – had someone from the hotel gone through my things and phoned the shop to tell them I had no pyjamas? That didn't make sense either, as many men do not bother wearing pyjamas and the hotel staff had no way of knowing whether I was one of these or not.

Yet again I found myself in the chemists without being aware of going there. This 'daydreaming' was going to have to stop. Here too I got exactly the same spiel as in the other shop, with the difference that the chemist had added a hairbrush I had forgotten to pack.

Back at the hotel I was greeted by a member of staff and told my lunch was waiting, the bellboy would take my 'purchases' to my room if I wished to go straight through, and 'no, the manager was out, but would be back in an hour or so'.

Seeing little else I could do, I sat down to a feast fit for a king, including wine that would have cost that king his whole ransom.

Between courses I took stock of all the weird things that were happening and realised I had overlooked an important one – here I was in a strange city, (in more ways than one), yet I had known where to find a clothes shop and chemist without a guidebook, map or having to ask directions.

The more I thought about it, the more I became convinced I was having a nervous breakdown. I was probably still at home asleep and having a dream, or maybe I was awake and had totally lost touch with reality. There simply wasn't any other plausible explanation.

I needed to test these theories to find out which was true, so I picked up a paper lying on the next table and looked at the date. It was today, not yesterday, so that ruled out my being still asleep and dreaming.

16

Next I phoned one of the staff who worked for my accountancy firm, asking if he had found a tax dodge for Mr Armbruster's accounts yet, and when he said he hadn't, I suggested he check the offshore accounts and compare them to Mr Alexander's as the same dodge may work for both. He did that while I waited, and found the same ploy would work - so that established that reality was still within my grasp – and got us another satisfied customer into the bargain, but got me no further forward in this puzzle.

Deciding to sit in my room and think a bit before doing anything else, I was on my way to the lift when the manager approached me saying, "The Sultan has requested an audience."

"The Sultan has requested an audience?"

"Yes. Perhaps he can clear up your other concerns."

"My other concerns?"

To his credit he gave no sign of noticing I had turned into a parrot, but rather continued, "He is waiting in the lounge. If you would like to go to your suite and freshen up I will ask him to go up in ten minutes."

"Thank you."

Like an obedient child I did as he suggested, and after a quick shower donned my trousers and shirt – jeans didn't seem appropriate for meeting a Sultan.

The Sultan of Pashima and a magnum of champagne arrived together, and after introductions he asked if I found his suite to my liking. I did of course, and told him so, explaining I thought I had only booked a normal room so it had been a lovely surprise.

"Ah!"

I sat like an idiot hoping he would clarify his exclamation which had sounded so full of meaning, but instead he asked, "And I suppose you thought you had booked to go to Spain too?"

"Yeeees?"

"Well you didn't. What you booked was our 'desperation holiday', *with all that entails*," he emphasised.

"What does it entail?"

There are two parts. The first is this; waving a careless hand around the suite; luxury and spoiling for you. The second is more complicated and does, I'm afraid, involve a decision from you.

Let me explain more – when someone behaves badly they get 'minus points' and the person they treat badly gets positive ones. Each set of points has a threshold – positive ones get you a sumptuous treat, negative ones earn you something negative.

While you are here you can ask for anything you want, anything at all. Whatever you choose can go back with you – it doesn't disappear once you leave here.

Or – you can choose to enjoy luxury surprises *we* choose for you, which only last however long you stay here - but, you get to choose your brother's punishment for his behaviour. That can also be anything at all. Anything! You must decide which of these you want within two minutes, but if you chose to be your brother's destiny, you have until dinner time to think of a punishment that would satisfy you."

I thought quickly – I did a job I loved helping people avoid taxes legally, and I owned my own, very successful company, so I could always buy my own 'treats'. However, the joy of watching my brother squirm, for the first time in my life, was worth more than any supercar or champagne.

"I want to choose his punishment."

"Very well. This afternoon, if you wish, you can play a round of golf with the world's number one, who will also give you tips and advice. Then you can have a sauna and massage before cocktails on the terrace. I will meet you for dinner and you can outline your plans for your brother's future."

To be honest I did not enjoy the golf as I was thinking of an adequate 'pound of flesh'. I had discarded having him killed, as I wanted to make him suffer, but that left lots of alternatives still open. I had little time to narrow them down and find the right one.

During a seven course feast I explained to the sultan that my brother's good position at work and consequent high social standing were more important to him than anything else. As he had twice stolen my most prized asset – love – I felt it was fitting he lose his job under some sort of cloud, and that would take care of his social aspirations too.

"That sounds reasonable. I will leave you to enjoy coffee and liqueurs as I must start the arrangements", said the sultan.

I thanked him and settled back replete, to my coffee, vintage brandy and hand rolled cigar, with a satisfied grin on my face.

I went to bed, slept long and deep and woke at noon – in my own house. The sultan was sitting in the lounge when I wandered through in a daze on my way to the kitchen.

"Why am I here?" I queried.

"It is all a misunderstanding," he replied to my short-lived relief. And after a pause he added, "Yours!"

"Huh?"

"You assumed the 'bad person' was your brother. You assumed you deserved indulgences and you assumed when I said people must pay, that did not include you. You assumed wrong."

"Taking you to my hotel I was offering you one last chance – you could gain anything or you could choose to hurt others. You choose to hurt, not only your brother, but your parents, your sister-in-law, your niece and your nephew. Did you think these people would care as little as you about what became of your brother?"

"It takes two to have sex, and while it was wrong of him, it was also wrong of the girls - and yes, it was them who approached him, just as he said, and not the other way round. When your brother asked for your help with his accounts many years ago, you charged him an exorbitant fee and stole money while you were doing them. You did the same to your parents – and your brother found out. He was hurt, but never said anything to your mother or father for fear of hurting them too, and that prompted him to accept the girls' offers of sex – to get even with you."

"On the holiday you took everything offered without really asking why and checking it was not a mistake. You went through the motions, so, if challenged you could say, "I did ask" but if you were really bothered you could have left money in the shop for the extra items, you could have suggested the suite was a mistake – you could have done much more, and you should have."

"We offered your brother the same deal as you - and he took 'gain'. He asked for forgiveness for what he had done - that is why the papers today are full of the scandal about how you embezzled funds and cheated your clients with various double deals and fraud."

"You chose your own fitting punishment."

Not Guilty

Shelia's Story

"Has the jury reached a verdict?"

"Yes. We find the defendant not guilty".

After those long wished for words I heard nothing else. The last few months had been a nightmare and there had been times I wondered if I would ever get my life back, but finally justice had prevailed and I could live again.

It had all started a year ago when my husband of two years had a small stroke. It totally changed his personality – everyone said so – but my life too might as well have ended that day, as it became intolerable for the next eight months. I tried to be patient with him, but there was so much more than patience required. He did weird things, and that meant keeping an eye on him all the time. No one knows what that means until they have been through it; it meant going everywhere with him, and if he got up in the night, which happened often, getting up too to be sure he didn't do anything foolish. It meant arguments with him to try and convince him to go to the supermarket with me, (something he hated), so he wouldn't be alone, having showers that lasted no longer than three minutes so he had no time to commit foolish acts, cooking food I could abandon in a hurry to stop him eating a glass or a knife.

This twenty-four hour surveillance may sound a bit difficult but it was only a part of the problem. Add to my lack of sleep and his wilful contrariness, the fact that whenever we were out in public he told everyone I beat him at home and kept him tied up. Anyone prepared to listen was told I was having affairs with the whole fire brigade, (including the women presumably), and poisoning his food.

People who had known him before we got married looked askew at me, some believing him totally and others showing doubt in the way they looked at and treated me. I couldn't blame them, as otherwise he seemed normal, and still showed great intelligence, but being seen as some sort of evil, sadistic, loose woman was not easy to take, especially as every waking moment was dedicated to him.

All in all it was a difficult time with a man I had not been married to for long, but I did feel I had taken him on whatever happened and luck was simply against me. Leaving him was not something I considered.

He had been a successful businessman who had moved into gold and silver investments for his clients and himself, but not satisfied with shares he had also fitted a safe in the house and filled it with bars and coins as well as bags of dust. One of his favourite new pastimes was to eat the dust, and as he was the only one who knew the combination of the safe, I couldn't get rid of this potential health hazard. I had tried asking a lawyer if there was any way I could get the safe opened and remove the dust, but as the house was in George's name only, I apparently did not have that legal right and the toxic dust stayed.

Eventually the silver dust got him. Ironic in some ways, as it really wasn't worth much, but apparently it was some sort of rare or special specimen, and that was why he kept it. What was left of it, and all the other really valuable stuff became mine, and there was rather a lot of it. I think that was why the police suspected me of killing him, (that and his continued assertions that I was poisoning him), as there was no other evidence against me.

During the trial witnesses were called who were his friends and had never been keen on me, so when they testified that they were at our home for a charity lunch one of the days he insisted I had him tied up and refused to give him lunch, but actually he had been at the table with them and had eaten with them, there was every reason to believe them. They also testified that the reason the meeting was in our home was because I didn't want to leave him alone, but as chairman of the board I needed to be at the meeting.

The lawyer I had contacted, asking if there was any way I could get the dust out of our house, also testified that I was worried and had tried to remove the danger but had legally been forbidden to do so.

The jury found me not guilty of either forcing him to eat the silver or of not preventing him. I was free and could get on with my life. Or so I believed that day.

Things were not that simple. Neighbours stared, whispered and crossed the street; colleagues from the soup kitchen I helped out at, found reasons not to work with me, although they had all been happy to come to our house to collect

22

huge pots of soup I made before the trial. The other charities I worked for found my help unnecessary and at the art gallery where I had bought quite a few paintings in the past, I found anything I liked was already sold – they had simply forgotten to put a red sticker on to indicate this. On it went, and I found things getting harder in the town that had been my husband's home but had never had the chance to become mine.

I had inherited quite a lot of money and decided I needed to use it to move to a place where no one knew who I was and start again. I could meet people who would be *my* friends and who actually liked me.

I packed a bag and drove south, stopping in small towns that looked interesting and staying in small hotels. There were many nice places, but none of them felt totally right; that indefinable but instant feeling of "this is it" was missing.

I found just the place after three days. It was a quaint old English village with a square and thatched cottages and real "leafy lanes". I stayed in the local inn, partly to be sure the place was suitable and partly to be sure that no one recognised me and I could be treated like a human being again. The answer to both these was an unequivocal yes, and to seal the deal, one day when I was walking down one of the leafy lanes, I came across a house for sale at the end of the road. The sign was hand written so I opened the gate and knocked at the door.

It was answered by a friendly widow who was selling due to the recent death of her husband. She invited me in and after the tour we sat in her kitchen and drank coffee. She talked about her husband who had been mugged and stabbed while abroad on business, and I said my husband had had a stroke which left him "not quite right" and he had eaten all sorts of odd things, one of which had killed him. I admitted I felt responsible for not stopping him and she reassured me I couldn't have avoided my doctor's appointment that day, (which was how he had time to consume so much of his precious dust).

I had known people would ask about my past sooner or later and it had to come out, so at least it was over and had gone well. I invited her to eat with me in the hotel that evening, and our friendship was born.

I bought her house and she moved to a smaller one in the village. She worked part time in the local post office and, following old traditions, was the local gossip, so having told her my sorry tale I didn't have to repeat it. The villagers got the story as they posted their letters and bought stamps.

At first I spent time refurbishing the house and decorating it, then landscaping the garden, but that done I needed something else to do. In a village like this there was little charity work to do and I preferred hands on work rather than fund raising at a distance, but there were a number of people of a certain age and I found nothing available to help them. I started a "Village Fare" charity and got a few locals on board. We took hot meals to elderly or ill people, did shopping or collected prescriptions for them and persuaded a car dealer to give us an old minibus that the local mechanic fixed free, under pressure, for days out to neighbouring towns.

The community accepted me willingly and soon I felt at home, and I was helping others. Life was pretty good. Then one day I took a frail old lady to the new doctor, (she didn't want to go as she only trusted the old one who had retired), and six months later I married the new doctor. He was wonderful with the old people and spent a long time reassuring them without losing patience. He sat listening to them reminisce while queues built up in his waiting room, and we often worked together to help them.

He had been terribly busy working since he arrived and for that reason he was still living in rented accommodation, therefore, after the wedding, he moved into my house as the simplest option.

Eighteen months passed in total bliss. It was one of those times when everything falls into your lap; parking spaces become vacant as you pull up, trains are five minutes late when you are running slightly behind, and all the things you want to buy are on offer. The few evenings I got home late James had food prepared, (he was a good cook), and a shaker of ice cold martini was waiting in the lounge. I thought maybe I was settled in married bliss for life – finally.

One evening I came back from visiting a lonely old man in hospital and James had changed. At the time he said nothing was wrong and nothing had happened, but much later on he told me the whole story.

James' Story

Shelia had just left to visit someone in hospital when there was a knock on the front door. I opened it and a tall serious man asked if I was Mr English and showed me his policeman's badge. Curious to hear the 'important thing' he had to tell me, I asked him in and offered him a glass of brandy. I only made the offer out of courtesy not expecting him to accept, but he did.

He took a sip and said he was not on duty but wanted to talk to me. He had information he felt it vital I know. The story he told was unbelievable, and the woman he talked about sounded nothing like the lady I had married. If the lawman were right, my wife had a past to rival Jack the Ripper's.

This is the story the inspector told.

Shelia married an eighty-seven year old man when she was nineteen. He died of a heart attack three days after the wedding, leaving her a very rich teenager. His children contested the will, but apart from labelling her a gold digger, nothing appeared out of the ordinary as her husband was not young and already had a heart condition when they married.

Shelia then left the small town where she had lived and moved to Manchester where she met and married a lawyer. He was killed in a hit and run accident a few years after the wedding. Shelia had organised a dinner party that night and six witnesses were waiting for him to get home while she plied them with cocktails and excuses. Again she inherited everything, as there were no children. No one dug into her background as her alibi was too good, and all the guests were respected members of the community.

Not long later she married a successful business owner who left her his business and considerable money when he died eleven months later. This time it was suicide – the classic car in the garage syndrome. She was at the theatre with friends, all pillars of society again, who were unshakeable in their statements that she spent the whole evening in their company. This time a good detective discovered this was her third husband to die shortly after putting a ring on her finger. Everything looked very suspicious but there was no proof and, based on the witnesses providing her with a perfect alibi, it seemed she could not have done it. The officers on the case thought she could have paid someone to do her dirty work, but there was no sign of a possible accomplice and no movement of money in her account that was unaccounted for. She was questioned, but never arrested. Although the policeman believed she did it, he had no idea how.

Husband number four was not as wealthy as the others but did already have a very large life insurance policy before she met him. He was a cautious accountant and, as well as making her beneficiary of the policy, he helped her invest her riches, which by now were considerable. He died by eating rat poison which he mixed into his food himself, in front of witnesses - while Shelia was in the bath. He had said jokingly, "I must take my medicine" before he did it but the people present thought it was all a joke and something other than rat poison was in the container - until he fell to the ground. By the time the ambulance got there it was too late.

By now we knew she had done it, but again couldn't prove anything. When we had to let her go I started to keep an eye on her whenever I could, knowing she would do it again.

The next one happened quickly. She met him and they were married after two months, and five months later he was dead. This time an accidental overdose was the cause. He was an addict, just like many pop stars, but generally wealthy people do not make that sort of mistake. It tends to happen more with low grade stuff or when an addict cannot afford to buy anything for a while, but none of these cases fit the rich and famous. Again Shelia had an alibi, which in itself is suspicious. Very few people will have an alibi for so many crimes - many are home alone, out walking alone, sleeping or something else where no one can see them.

The one before you was a stock broker who ate silver dust which killed him. She stood trial for that, which was a first, but again she had an unshakeable alibi and got off.

I just wanted you to know who you had married, and I seriously doubt she told you any of this. I can see by your expression I was right about that, but I can also see you do not believe it, which is unfortunate. She is an extraordinarily intelligent woman and each murder was different, but make no mistake, they were all murdered. You will be too and probably soon, so be very careful. Check old newspapers if you do not believe me, (each death was reported and your wife was nicknamed the 'House Hunter' as she got so many new homes with each death), but I would advise against saying anything to her. She may feel threatened if you know, and strike before you have figured out what she is going to do.

I would like you to come with me now, but if you won't do that, think carefully of some excuse to leave in a day or two, and if you need any help in the meantime, give me a call at this number. (He handed me his card.) We have no idea how she does it, or who her accomplice is – it could be a man or woman, and that means we can't protect you and you may not see it coming. You cannot stay here with her, I hope you see that.

I pointed out that I loved her very much, and the woman he described was not the caring human being I had married. I said I needed to think, adding I would call if necessary, and reluctantly he showed himself out.

I sat without moving until she came home, but even then I was too shocked to act normally and rushed off to bed to avoid talking to her. I got up early next morning and left before she woke, but I knew I had to face her soon, probably that evening, although I had no idea what to say or how to behave.

Shelia and James' Story

Life wasn't easy for a week or so with James doing everything he could to avoid Shelia, and she wondering what was wrong, (although being found out did not cross her mind, such was her high opinion of herself).

However, as time passed and nothing untoward occurred James began to feel a bit easier. Maybe there was nothing to worry about after all, and soon they got back to a more normal life, but he kept an eye on her just the same, wondering if she were going to do something and what it could be.

The only factor all the deaths seemed to have in common was her absence along with a strong alibi, so whenever she said she was meeting friends for lunch, he turned up unexpectedly, and if she were going out in the evenings he started to accompany her, using the excuse he worried about her safety after dark. James struggled to believe his wife was a murderess, and anyway all those dead husbands had been rich, while James was most definitely not, but try as he might to dismiss the idea, something niggled.

James felt he was coming across as loving and caring, but Shelia felt he was becoming excessively jealous and cloying, but neither confronted the other.

Then things started to change, subtly, but he noticed. She, who had always been so punctual, came back later in the evenings with no explanation, other than she had lost track of time. He worried she was planning his death and spent hours in his study thinking about what to do.

One evening Shelia made him dinner, and when he got to the table there was only one place set and she was wearing her coat.

"I am just nipping out to visit Mrs Catlin. She had a bad fall and I want to be sure she doesn't need anything", she said and left before he had time to suggest going too.

In panic James called the inspector, who told him to put the food into a bag, go to the local hotel and wait in the bar. When the policeman arrived he took the bag for analysis and again said James needed to leave.

"But what if you are wrong and she is innocent?" was James' reply.

"I'm not, and she isn't."

"But she might be. You said there was no way she could have done any of them, so maybe it really is a series of coincidences."

"It isn't. You are in mortal danger, and if you did not believe it possible, why are we sitting here with your dinner in a shopping bag?"

"I love her."

And again that ended the discussion.

Dinner proved harmless and James felt foolish. He tried to make it up to Shelia by making extra special martinis. She loved them and he made it his mission to please and surprise her with new twists. He invented a lemon martini with a splash of lemon juice, followed by a lime one, and that led to what turned out to be her favourite, a grapefruit one.

A few weeks before their second wedding anniversary Shelia announced she was organising a special party to celebrate, but refused to tell him any details, saying it was to be a surprise.

James knew instinctively this was to be it and sat in his surgery thinking about all the ways it could happen, even as his patients explained their illnesses he imagined poisoned food, spiked drinks, chandeliers falling on his head and all manner of other possible but improbable things. Everything seemed too chancy – someone else might eat or drink the poison, and he may not be standing under the chandelier at the right time.

She made furtive arrangements, under the guise of creating a mysterious spectacle for him, but he overheard snippets of conversation, (eavesdropped actually), and phrases like "it must be exactly on time otherwise all our efforts will have been wasted. It is vital you time it to the second", seemed to confirm what he suspected.

He invited the inspector to the party as an "old university chum", and for the first time began to have doubts about staying with her, but they never lasted long. He always came back to the same thought, "It took me so long to find her I can't leave her. My life would be worthless without her. Nothing would matter."

One day he came home early and entered silently to discover Shelia in the kitchen with a caterer, and before she saw him, he heard, "You do understand that plate is for my husband only. Nothing will work if some idiot serves it to another person by mistake."

He backed up and opened the front door, closing it loudly, before shouting, "I'm home darling. Where are you?"

He now believed he knew how it would happen and that meant he could avoid it, so, if he managed to spill the food without eating it, everything could return to the way it was and he could carry on as if nothing had happened.

No sooner had he relaxed, than later that same evening he heard her in the kitchen making dinner and talking on the phone. He crept over to the door and listened, "…. and it must happen while we are all watching the fireworks. I will be standing beside my husband and will have our local celebrity, Lady Horton, on my left. When I suggest she might see better from my position and we swap places, that is when you must do it – not before. Is that clear?"

He started to sweat and sat down feeling nauseous. Another possibility! He could avoid this too by moving when she swapped places, but if there were two possible scenarios then there could be three – or more. Maybe that was her trick, having multiple accomplices and different possibilities, so she really didn't know when or how it would happen.

When she hung up he called the house using his mobile phone and answered quickly before she had time to pick up the phone. Then he rushed into the kitchen saying in agitation, "that was an emergency, I have to go out."

He was gone inside a few seconds, with no coat, and more interestingly to Shelia, with no medical bag.

Shelia had a glass of wine in the kitchen as she tried to slow down dinner so he would find a good meal ready whatever time he came back and pondered this. What did it mean? Did he suspect? No, impossible. She had decided a while ago he must have seen or heard something that made him think she was being unfaithful. That explained his sudden jealousy and odd behaviour, but as she wasn't having an affair, and hadn't even considered it, she was at a loss to think what could have triggered this idea.

Her being unfaithful did not explain this evening though, but then she hit on an idea; he was probably organising a special surprise for her - something for their party that Friday, and as men were notoriously clumsy in their efforts at hiding surprises that explained his odd behaviour. But on the off chance he did suspect, she would need to be careful and be sure to make no wrong moves.

James drove to a car park, parked the car and sat thinking. He imagined his return home. "How was your emergency, and who was ill?" As he tried to think of an answer he realised he had not taken his bag. Damn. That ruined everything, and he mustn't make her suspicious otherwise she might do it sooner and he would not be ready for it.

He made a quick decision. He would call the inspector and suggest he arrive early for the party so 'two old friends could have a quick drink and catch up on news'. He would have a bag packed and leave with the policeman before the party began. That only left this evening and tomorrow to get through.

He noticed the supermarket beside the car park was still open and dashed inside where he bought a big box of chocolates, several bunches of flowers and a bottle of perfume.

Back home he said, "Sorry for the deception, but a wave of love so strong hit me and I just had to go out and get you these immediately."

Shelia was delighted and laughed.

They had a lovely evening – he thinking about what to pack and she feeling smug with the knowledge that once again she had chosen well. He was too stupid and loved her too much to suspect anything.

The next day James phoned the lawman from his clinic to explain his decision and ask for help.

The inspector again asked James why he would not leave there and then, but the doctor replied that he had asked himself the same thing. He thought the answer was that it was partly to do with pride that he wished for the party to go ahead, and partly due to his doctor's training he wanted to help if there was a chance the police could catch her and stop her doing it again.

The arrangements were made for early next evening, with the inspector agreeing that the party was the perfect cover for Shelia to put any plan into action and saying he believed James may be safe until then.

James had already instructed his receptionist not to make appointments for the day of the party, explaining he had secret things to organise for his wife, but no one must know he wasn't working. He sat in his office terrified. It was so risky. What if he had calculated wrong? What if she killed him before the policeman arrived? There were so many things that could go wrong, with such drastic consequences, he wondered if he should just walk away, but discarded this alternative almost immediately. He had waited this long and come so far - he could not give up now.

All day he worried and suffered terrible dread about the evening, but at four o'clock he left and went home as planned. He had a quick shower and changed, and then while Shelia was getting dressed he made an extremely large shaker of martinis. He downed a couple in quick succession to calm his nerves, and waited for her. Into the room swept a vision of loveliness and radiance. He was shocked at her appearance, as never before had she shone like this. He realised it was the thrill of the hunt and that it was not only about money, but that she enjoyed the kill and the hairs on the back of his neck stood up. Any remaining doubt lifted in that instant and he saw her in the same light as the policeman, for the first time.

His blood ran cold and he nearly got cold feet, wishing to flee there and then, but unsure how to do it.

Getting himself back under control with difficulty he suggested a quiet, romantic drink before the crowd arrived. One last drink together with his beautiful wife. He proudly presented Shelia with his new martini, invented in her honour, and with secret ingredients. James showed her how much he had made, pressing the shaker into her hands, while raising an empty glass in salute, and, laughingly said, "Want to drink it straight from there? Saves time!"

Laughing too, she poured the drink into two glasses, and then taking one sat down in an armchair smiling, while he took the other before choosing the armchair opposite hers.

"A mystery, eh?" she enquired after the first sip. "I love it."

"I have been working on it for ages. I called it the 'Anniversary Special', in honour of us.

She drank it and asked for another.

"I think not", he replied, setting his own glass down with a smile. "One is sufficient."

"Sufficient for what?" Shelia asked.

"To kill you my dear."

"What!"

32

"I am a doctor and have been developing a poison that is tasteless but strong - just for this purpose."

She made as if to rise, but apart from placing her hands on the arms of the chair nothing else happened.

"It paralyses from the legs up, slowly but effectively. You will not die for ten or fifteen minutes, but as it reaches your lungs they will stop working. I wanted this time to have a talk."

"How did you do all those murders, I am curious." He inquired.

At first she denied everything, but as time wore on and she got slowly worse, he admitted he had also made an antidote which could be hers if she told the truth. She eventually admitted it all.

It really was very simple. Shelia had learnt to hypnotise people, and all the witnesses had been chosen for their receptiveness to her ability. She had hypnotised some into believing she was with them when actually she wasn't. She had also used the same power to convince one husband to eat rat poison, another to take too many drugs and so on. There was no accomplice; it was all sleight of hand, so to speak.

"And how was I to be dispatched?"

"You weren't. I loved you."

"But the party – the plate 'only for me' and the 'thing' that was to happen during the fireworks?"

"The plate held a beautiful brown leather and red gold Baume et Mercier Hampton watch, and during the fireworks they were going to deliver the key to a safety deposit box that contains all the gold, silver and palladium my last husband left me. I wanted you to have your own money."

He sat stunned for a few minutes digesting this before asking if it were all true.

Finding it was, by the simple matter of going into the kitchen where the said plate waited, and picking up the watch, (she was right it was lovely), he returned to her.

"Time is running out. In a couple of minutes you will find it hard to breathe." As he spoke he picked up his glass from beside his chair and poured something into it from a small bottle. He held it out towards her, saying it was the antidote, but before she could drink it he took it back and drank it himself.

As she looked in astonishment he said, "I lied. There is no antidote."

"With effort, as by now the end was closing in fast, she asked why.

"You never did meet your first husband's grandson did you? He was away in America studying to become a doctor."

Her eyes opened wide but by now she was unable to speak. He continued, "I came home for the funeral but my flight was delayed and I missed it. I had intended to go back to America, but my family were very distressed and there was a lot to sort out, so I ended up staying. When I heard your next husband died I started to follow your career and the idea hit me. It took a while to develop the poison, but when I was ready I arranged to meet you, and let's be honest, by then you were very wealthy and any husband who managed to outlive you would inherit it all – so here I am. The inspector happened along by chance, but his presence will work nicely to my advantage."

He just managed to finish his sentence before she left the earth she had used so badly.

His timing was impeccable, and as he placed the glass in his hand back on the small table beside his chair, the doorbell rang.

He didn't answer it. It rang again. He didn't move. Next thing the inspector and two uniformed policemen rushed into the room to see him sitting with his head in his hands and Shelia dead.

"What happened?" demanded the long arm of the law.

34

"We were having a pre-party drink. Shelia prepared it, and as I always do now, I switched her glass for mine without her noticing, not really because I thought there was anything in it, but by now it was a habit."

"Then ………." "Oh …………." "Oh my God!" "Sheliaaaaa!"

"Don't worry Sir, it wasn't your fault. That was meant for you, there is no doubt about that," the policeman comforted.

When we analyse the shaker and find her prints, with yours on top, along with the prints on the glasses, that will be conclusive enough – especially when put together with her history.

That was what I had counted on, and why I wiped the shaker before she arrived.

Back in Time

As she waited looking out over the Bay of Silence, her thoughts turned to Shelley, Byron and Hans Christian Andersen. These thoughts were not as random as they might appear, for all of these writers had stayed here in the past and one bay on this promontory was named in honour of Andersen, "The Bay of Fables", while this one was called Portobello, otherwise known as the Bay of Silence.

Sitting on a rock overlooking the bay she felt a cold breeze, and saw a vivid scene, as if it were portrayed on the surface of the turquoise water - it was as though she were watching a cinema screen.

She was a twenty year old girl, over two centuries ago in the early eighteen hundreds, and was running down the narrow cobbled street where all the shops were. It was early in the morning, and many shopkeepers were outside working on their pavement displays. Some greeted her by name and others offered brioche for breakfast as she passed, but today she had no time to stop. On she ran, until she reached the small street almost hidden between two old buildings and, taking this she continued past the Bay of Silence, and into the convent on the headland.

There was no one around to stop her and she knew exactly the place she wanted. Up in the high room she rushed to the window and waited, trying to catch her breath, but before that happened she saw the signal and knew what it meant.

Taking a deep breath she went back down to the bay where she dived fully clothed into the warm water and swam straight across the short stretch of crystal clear water.

On the other side she climbed the hill and went through the friary gates. Unaware of the magnificent view of the two bays this vantage point offered, she met the monk who gave her the key to her future. At the time she didn't know what it meant, knowing only it was very important, but he assured her she would understand when she returned. Then, heart pounding and legs trembling, she went back down and returned to the main thoroughfare, her clothes already drying in the warm sun. Going as fast as she could she passed all the buildings with the painted on, pretend windows and painted cornerstones until, nearly at the other end, she saw the tall red library long before she reached the heavy wooden entrance that would take her to her destiny.

Without pausing she pushed open the door and climbed the steps. Carlo was waiting for her, and as they embraced he said, "You know I love you and you are my world. Have you no bag? Did you forget it?"

"I had trouble getting away and couldn't bring it," she replied.

"Never mind we can buy you more clothes when we are far away and finally married."

Sighing as her story came to a happy ending she sensed her husband beside her. She had not felt him arrive and he had not spoken until now. Then Carlo said, "You know I love you and you are my world. Have you no bag? Did you forget it?"

"You were miles away when I arrived," he continued before she could reply.

"No, I was years away, but still in Sestri Levante," she answered.

Steam Train

I was lucky to be born with the proverbial silver spoon clamped firmly in my jaws. This spoon held a large amount of money in the bank and a thriving business, run efficiently and effectively by a team of managers and directors.

This allowed me to do whatever I wanted. I took the odd trip into the office to keep an eye on things and the rest of the time I did charity work, played tennis, went sailing and generally had a good time.

I lived in a house in town; actually it was more of a mansion, and had been in my family for generations, and my great-great- something grandfather, a wily old fox, had given a large part of what was originally the garden to the city as a public park. He had given the land "for the use of", retaining ownership, but the city ran and maintained the park on the condition it was free for anyone to use.

I loved steam trains and was fascinated by them, but had no particular desire to be a real steam train driver. Then one day I hit on the idea of combining my interest in trains with my charity work and decided to build a small model railway in the park. As the land was now mine, this was a simple matter and required no bureaucratic form filling, so was done quite quickly with courtesy calls to the city officials to ask them if they thought it a good idea. As I was paying for it, organising it and running it, they did all think it great. The idea was; it was free for the children to use and the members of the charity I had set up took turns driving the train at weekends.

It was a great success and the kids loved it – so did I. In theory it was open on Saturday and Sunday afternoons but I often went there in the mornings too, and if any children wished - I drove them round the architectural wonder that was the track. The journey took about twenty minutes and had a long tunnel, a gentle hill, a low valley and even a station half way round where more children could join the ride or parents could meet the ones on the train. We set up an ice-cream and sweet stall there as well, and if children wanted they could get off, buy something and get back on. There was also a coffee shop for parents, and quadraphonic speakers blasted fun music for all ages to boost a holiday type mood.

One Saturday morning I went to the park as usual and found a sad looking boy standing staring at the train. He was alone and dressed in rags, (old scuffed shoes, muddy trousers with a hole in one knee and a shirt with frayed cuffs). I went over to speak to him asking if he was lost, but he shook his head and pointed to a lady talking to a man close by. I assumed she was his mother, meaning he wasn't lost, so asked if he liked trains. He nodded. Would he like a ride, I ventured, and this produced another nod, so I told him to check with his mother and climb on board, and I got into the drivers cockpit to wait for him.

We set off, him a lonely figure in the carriage. This was unusual as normally when the engine started a stream of excited children ran up and jumped in. We went into the big tunnel and as we were going through it I started to feel funny. Not ill, just strange. We deliberately had not lit the tunnel to make it more exciting for the kids, but today I missed illuminations and wished I could see. I had driven through here hundreds of times without feeling like this and couldn't understand what was wrong, but as I contemplated this we emerged once again into bright sunlight.

Anxious about the odd sensations, I immediately looked round. The boy was sitting there, just as he had been before. "Everything OK?" I shouted. He nodded.

I looked down at myself; my muted red wool broadcloth coat with white satin lapels was impeccable, my high-ish standing collar was still standing up well, my double-breasted black waistcoat with red embroidery looked good, my cream cotton corduroy knee breeches had no stains, my shoes shone and most importantly, reaching up I felt my cravat was still tied to perfection.

I looked around; people were walking unconcerned, children and dogs were playing while riders and phaetons were doing the rounds unperturbed and ladies with taffeta gowns, matching hats and parasols were promenading with very high-collared dandies. All looked tranquil, but I knew that was not the case. The problem was, what could I do about it – walk up to people and say, "Something is wrong." The first thing they would ask was, "What?" and I had no answer to that. I decided the only thing to do was carry on as normal until I saw someone who looked as mystified as I felt, meaning they had sensed it too. I couldn't be the only one.

That was what I did, and when I stopped at the station on the other side I expected more children to climb aboard. I jumped out and bought the lad in my train an ice-cream, as I knew from his appearance he would not have money for such treats, and on returning to the train I expected to see it had filled up, but it hadn't.

Sitting all alone was the youngster, and on receiving the delight he managed to speak long enough to say "Thank you", before tucking in.

I went back to the engine and drove back to the start, where he got off, gave me another "Thank you Sir", and disappeared.

Totally unsettled, I shut off the engine and went home, wondering about Thomas, the man who was to drive it this afternoon; would he feel it too, or was I the only one?

Even my home looked unfamiliar and the servants looked different, but they treated me the same as always and provided an excellent repast of my favourite dishes for lunch.

I felt as if I had been drugged and taken to a new place where everything was familiar but different, brighter somehow. Things were not right, but in such a way I couldn't figure out what was wrong. I knew there was a problem, but couldn't find it and it was really starting to drive me insane. I spent the rest of the weekend at home pondering what had happened and how I felt, but got more questions than answers, so to keep my mind off something I seemed to have no control over, I needed to go to work. Perhaps there things would feel normal again, or maybe I could even get some answers.

On Monday I went into the office and went straight into the manager's office. He looked different too so I asked, "Fredrick Junior?"

"Bless you Sir, but let me get married before you start giving me children."

I thought I had cured him of calling me Sir, as in this day and age titles were not what they used to be, but it seemed he had lapsed into old ways. Even his answer seemed odd to me, but again there was little I could really fault – he was called Fredrick after some ancient relative and the 'junior' had been tagged on by the family so they knew which one they were talking about, but as this Fredrick

40

had no children and was engaged, his answer was correct, but still didn't fit with the man I knew.

I asked about business and he told me that in 'Izzy', one of our old emerald mines in South Africa, they had found a new lode. We thought the mine had been emptied years ago, and I wasn't aware we were still exploring it, and just as I was about to ask why I had not been informed of the activity there, in rushed a messenger. He handed the telegram to Fredrick, who passed it unopened to me.

"Found large pebble Stop Diamond Stop One inch Stop Advise Stop"

Speechless, I handed it back to Fredrick who also stood in silence.

Eventually I rallied and said, "We need to answer".

Fredrick got a quill pen and wrote 'Find more Stop'.

"That do?" he asked, and when I replied it would suit very well, he handed it to the boy along with a sovereign.

"We will have to find out what De Beer's policy is", I said.

"Who's he?"

"The company", I responded in astonishment. I would have expected a good business manager to at least know the name, but again, as we did not deal with diamonds, there was no good reason why he should.

I left then as Fredrick had a lot to organise if we were to make another fortune in diamonds, and I fancied a celebratory bottle of bubbly rather than writing endless reports. Before leaving I cautioned him to check with De Beers about rights, permission and so forth, and his admonition not to worry as he always double checked every move before making it, left me feeling foolish. He was right, I couldn't have wished for a better manager.

All that week the odd sensation stayed with me, and as time wore on I realised more and more I didn't fit there, I shouldn't be there, but where I should be or how to get there remained elusive.

I got through the week without being conscious of what I did – I think there was a dinner party and a picnic, and I know I played tennis, but that is all that I am aware of.

Saturday morning arrived bright and sunny in direct contrast to my dark feelings. For the first time since building the railway I did not want to go to the park and drive the train, but a nagging feeling plagued me, that as all this had started there and therefore, maybe the answer lay there too, I put on my best frock coat and left.

The same urchin was standing in the same place but I didn't see his mother, although I didn't remember her that clearly as I had been more intent on pleasing the boy.

We went through the same rigmarole with me asking if he wanted a ride, him nodding and both of us getting onto the train with no other passengers following suit, just like the last time. I asked if his mother knew where he was and that gained me yet another nod. Apprehensive, we set off and approached the tunnel and for some reason I braced myself. Going through it I felt exactly the same as before – weird and in need of light, but just like the last time we came out both apparently unscathed.

I checked he was fine and then looked at myself; maroon coat - check; black shirt - fine; red designer jumper - yes; cream cords were properly creased and clean; trainers clean and knots tied; and my scarf was still round my neck.

Looking round I saw everyone having a good time and the obligatory smart phones and tablets were in full use as people took pictures of anything and everything, including the train.

When I got back home I saw something that had been missing over the past week – a photo. It showed my great-great-grandfather sitting in the garden, and working in the background was the gardener with his son standing beside him. I vaguely recalled the story of how the boy had drowned in the pond when he was very young, but could remember no details. The gardener's son was a small boy with old scuffed shoes, muddy trousers with a hole in one knee and a shirt with frayed cuffs and a face I recognised.

A Body in the Lane

One day, while out walking with my cat, I found a dead body.

This may sound odd from all perspectives, but I had a cat who enjoyed going for a walk with me and we made a point of doing it every day. I lived in the country in a remote area, so going for a walk was a pleasure. There were various routes to choose from and on none of them did I meet any traffic except an occasional tractor. The road was tarred as far as my house, but about twenty yards further on it became a dirt track and at that point it went rapidly up a hill and down again and it was about half a mile after the hill we found the body.

Going for long walks was not Chloe's only peculiarity, she also communicated with me all day long. She meowed when she wanted food, she had a different meow when she wanted to go for a walk, and yet another indicated she wanted to be let out. During our walks she always stayed with me, only leaving me once during each walk to go to the toilet. She used whichever field was nearest when she felt the urge and once finished, she came straight back to join me and continue the walk. She had never deviated from this so, that day when she stayed in the field, calling me with an odd desperate sounding meow that I had never heard before, I immediately assumed there was a problem. A hedge was blocking her from my view so I climbed the gate to get into the field and see what her problem was; imagining a fox or something else was threatening her.

She was sitting beside a male body, lying flat out on his back and turned slightly towards the field, with his eyes open. I had never touched a dead body and didn't really want to start, so I gently touched the man with my toe and feeling a hard, rocklike resistance, thought it was the police I needed to call, as it was too late for an ambulance. The fixed eyes had made him look dead, but having no experience in this area, I had wanted to be sure there was nothing I could do to help him.

The police asked me to wait there until they arrived, and to pass the time I had a good look at him from where I was standing. I didn't move around much, so as not to make too many footprints, and I didn't touch anything – I even picked Chloe up so she would not walk on vital evidence. At first he seemed normal, which was why it was not upsetting to look at him, but after a while I saw a small hole in the breast pocket of his jacket. The material of his suit was dark, so I couldn't be sure, but it did look as if the hole had a dark ring round it which could have been blood.

This made me uncomfortable as I wondered if it was a bullet wound – and that meant murder. I took an involuntary step back and looked around me. Silly really, as the murderer, if it was murder, would have disappeared as soon as I arrived, either that or shot me too to stop me calling the police. I moved away from the cadaver and had a brief look around to see if there was a gun nearby, but saw nothing.

I waited at the gate for what seemed like ages and as the arrival of dark clouds threatened a downpour, I had the idea that perhaps I should take photos of the body so the police could see how he was lying and look at any other details they wanted. If it did rain heavily it may wash something vital away, and it couldn't do any harm to snap a few shots. I went back into the fields and took half a dozen shots from a distance, and more up close, then retreated to wait in the lane again. I always took my phone with me on these walks to jot down ideas for my writing if they came to me, and as this seemed like a good idea for a book, I wrote a description of everything I saw to pass the time.

As it turned out later, it was lucky I took the pictures, because what happened next was not the professional and organised thing that happens in films. There were a lot of policemen just wandering aimlessly around leaving footprints, and as they say in the movies, "contaminating evidence".

The officers agreed he was dead, declaring he had been dead for at least a few days, and then asked me who he was, insisting I must have seen him around. Why they thought I would know was a mystery, and as they did not inspire confidence, I just hoped they wouldn't decide I had killed a man I had never seen before. There seemed to be little investigating going on, and if they wanted a suspect, I was the only person available.

They asked if had I touched or removed anything, which seemed ridiculous considering the first policeman into the field had rolled the body right over, poked and prodded and had searched all the cadaver's clothes without bothering to look at how he was placed. I had watched the search and was surprised to find every

44

pocket was empty; no money, no keys, no phone, (and a person who wore clothes like those seemed likely to have a phone with them twenty four hours a day), but he still had his watch on. A Rolex, no less.

I told them I had only pushed him gently with my toe and, as it has still not rained, I didn't mention the photos, which now seemed a bit ghoulish – I reckoned they could take their own if they wished, although from their indifference, this seemed unlikely to happen. If they asked how he was lying later on I could give them the pictures, but maybe the first policeman had taken in the scene better than I thought in the few seconds before he moved the body.

They asked me to stay there so they could ask me more questions, but the time I had already spent standing there waiting for them had caused an old back injury to flare up, so I told them where I lived and said I would wait at home. I didn't know anything and had already repeated my one sentence about finding him five or six times, but if I could help with anything else, I would.

I left them to it and wandered home, telling Chloe she was a clever girl for calling to show me the man. Without really being aware I was addressing my remarks to a cat, I speculated on who he was and what he was doing there.

He was olive skinned, like men from the Mediterranean often were, although here in Ireland there is an occasional person who has that colouring, so it didn't necessarily mean he was foreign. He was dressed in obviously expensive clothes, and this was so out of place in the middle of the country, that must mean something significant. His suit appeared to be classy; well cut; nice material and beautiful lining; his tie looked like silk, but his shoes clinched it for me. They were loafers and had the distinctive horse's bit and logo that showed them to be Gucci. Why would anyone dressed like that be walking in a remote area of countryside with no car visible anywhere nearby? I intended to ask the police to let me know who he was and what he was doing here, as this piqued my curiosity. It felt wrong – it was wrong.

The police didn't come to my house for many long hours and even then it was only to say goodbye. My interest had built considerably in that time and I managed to tempt them in with the offer of a cup of tea. Using the time they were there to try and get some information, I asked if the hole was a bullet and they said yes. One of them even told me they thought it was suicide, without my having to ask.

"Had they found the gun?" I asked and when they replied they hadn't, I only just managed to refrain from saying, "How did a man who had just shot himself manage to hide a gun? And how many suicide victims shoot themselves in the heart?" They had obviously thought about the missing gun, as again the information was volunteered that "someone must have taken it, along with his wallet".

Now that just sounded too stupid to be true and this time I didn't manage to keep my mouth shut.

"Who could have taken it? I am a ghost writer and I work from home. (I could see from their expressions they thought I wrote about ghosts, so quickly explained I wrote things other people pass off as their own.) My desk, as you can see, faces the road and I see most of the traffic that goes that way. Granted I may have been in the kitchen or another room when someone passed and missed seeing them, but this area is so remote no one even knows it exists – and you could not see him from the road, so no one could have known the gun was there! Also who steals money and leaves a Rolex?"

I got a patronising, "Leave it to the professionals", and again resisted saying, "Fine, where are they?" as further communication with these idiots seemed pointless.

The police left, agreeing to let me know if they found out anything, including his identity, but I had little faith in their ability and thought this mystery might just stay a mystery if they were the only hope of discovering the truth. They just didn't seem interested in doing anything.

Their reaction when I said I was a ghost writer was surprising and worrying. Firstly, I didn't think my profession was so obscure that out of a group of five people, none would know what it was. Secondly, writing about ghosts would make me a 'writer of ghost stories', and not a 'ghost writer'. Lastly, and perhaps the most important point, even if I did write about ghosts that did not make me a dangerous witch. They had all looked uncomfortable with the thought and had given each other that knowing look that says, "She is nuts. Let's get out of here before she turns us into toads." It was a very old fashioned and narrow minded way of thinking and totally unsuited to any investigating. However, not being a witch, there was nothing I could do about it, but speculate as to who the man was and what he was doing there.

Over the next few days Chloe and I took other routes for our walks, but the next time we went down that path Chloe did the same thing again, this time a few fields down and on the other side. When she called me from the field I actually felt sick, fearing another body, but after climbing the gate I couldn't find anything. She kept insisting something was wrong, so I looked until I found a briefcase in the ditch. It had been partly covered with grass and when I pulled it out it was immediately obvious it was a very good quality case. I assumed it belonged to the body and hesitated, unsure if it were better to leave it in the field or take it home. After much tribulation, I thought that as I had removed it from its hiding place I might as well take it home.

It was locked, (I did try), but I had often opened my own case with a wire, as I frequently mislaid the keys, so I assumed I could easily spring this lock too. The problem was that I might scratch the lock and the police would notice, so I left it closed and phoned the police like a good citizen.

I couldn't remember the name of the man in charge, so asked the receptionist for anyone working on the "mysterious body in the lane". She asked my name and reason for calling, but her manner and words, as she told me they probably did not have time to waste talking to me, got my back up. Instead of saying what I had intended, "I found a briefcase and think it belongs to the body", I said, "I have an important clue". This sounded more dramatic, I thought, and I didn't want her to know about the new evidence - silly I know.

She told me to "hold" and a few seconds later came back after talking to someone, but as she had not covered the receiver I had heard the whole conversation. She said someone would call me later that day, but I had heard a man reply, "Tell her to sod off and stop bothering us. It's probably the only excitement she gets."

Although I was sure no one was going to call, I waited all that day just in case I was wrong, with the briefcase constantly tormenting me from the chair I had set it on. That evening, after no phone call had been forthcoming, I got a small piece of wire and within ten minutes the lock popped open.

Excited, I opened it, took a photo before removing anything, and proceeded to set all the contents on the table. On top was a phone, a wallet and car keys, (they had the Audi symbol on the keys, so no great detective work required there), some documents in French and a tablet computer. A packet of Gitanes cigarettes and gold Dunhill lighter more or less confirmed something I had already thought – this was a vain man. He probably kept his phone and cigarettes in his case so they would not ruin the line of his suit, even though it was not a convenient arrangement. (I had come across this same vanity many times during my travels in Italy). It also appeared to settle the question of his dark skin - he must be French. No Irishman would carry a pile of French documents without a translation in English and very few could stomach the strong, inimitable taste of Gitanes. His wallet held only money and no clue as to his identity. The money was mainly Euro, but there were a few notes in other currencies too, mainly dollars and sterling, but that didn't really seem significant.

Hoping the phone and tablet were charged I tried turning them on. The phone steadfastly showed a blank screen, but the computer obliged. I tried fitting both gadgets with my own chargers and luckily they all used the same micro USB attachment. I left the phone to charge as I tried to figure out how to work the tablet. I didn't know the make and it was showing everything in French, which made it difficult. My schoolgirl French was not good enough to let me figure out how to work this computer, but I hit on the idea of searching on the internet for an English manual for this machine using my own laptop.

I got the language on the tablet changed into English, and that hurdle overcome, things went better. I couldn't make head or tail of the stuff on it as it was all in French, but there was a calendar and the last entry was for two days before I found him and said, "Meet beneficiary of P's will. Get signature quickly!" I checked the translation on a few internet translators and it always came up with the same result. To be honest I hadn't expected anything so cryptic and was surprised, and delighted, that my imagination seemed to be running parallel with real life.

I wondered how long he had been dead. Had he kept the appointment or been killed first? (I was in no doubt he had been murdered. Apart from the missing gun, who would throw their briefcase into a field, then field to commit suicide?)

I searched the tablet but found nothing more I could use, so I waiteu ~ phone had enough charge to use, then I looked at his last calls and found the number he called most frequently was someone called Jacques. I dialled the number and a Frenchman answered almost immediately. I asked if he spoke English, and luckily he did.

I asked him if he knew the man whose phone I was using and to describe him. The description fitted perfectly, right down to the tiny scar at the corner of his right eye, so I explained what had happened. I told him the police had refused to take my call about the briefcase, so I had opened it and found the phone number. Jacques was the dead man's associate and friend and he had been worried something had happened as he had heard nothing from his friend for a few days. They were both French lawyers and the cadaver was called Alain.

Jacques, enigmatically, did not want to say any more on the phone, but arranged to meet me in London airport the next day. He counselled caution, as he too believed Alain had been murdered and, because I was involved, he felt I was in danger.

I didn't sleep that night, partly from excitement and partly fear but, buoyed by the anticipation of unravelling this mystery, I started out early the next morning and caught the shuttle to London. I got to the designated meeting place, a café, first and having described myself to Jacques on the phone, waited for him to find me. It was about an hour later before Jacques appeared, and he wanted a cup of coffee before talking to me. The queue was long and my curiosity was driving me insane, nevertheless I had no choice but to wait the extra ten minutes.

Sitting down, Jacques said he would like to ask me a few questions before he answered mine and added they were extremely important, maybe even a question of life or death.

Intrigued I told him to go ahead. I had already told him everything I knew on the phone, so there were only a few questions left I wanted to ask, such as why Alain was there, and the answer to that might come out along with his questions.

"Did Alain contact you?" was his first question.

"No."

"Do you know Marcel Picard?"

"I don't know him, but I know of him. He is the famous watch maker who died recently. What does he have to do with this?" I asked uncomprehendingly.

"Patience, I am almost finished. Do you know who your paternal grandmother Margaret's sisters were?"

"I didn't even know she had more than one sister. She died when I was very young and no one really talked about her, but her sister Willamina was considered a "bad lot" and no one had contact with her. I never met her or her family," I replied, astonished at having unknown relatives.

"Ah, I see. Then before you ask me questions, and I can see you have many, there is something I must tell you. Jennifer, your grandmother's sister ran off and married a Frenchman when she was young and her family were very upset about this. She was engaged to a Lord at the time and it caused quite a scandal. Jennifer was eighteen and your grandmother fourteen when it happened. Willamina was only eight. At first Jennifer wrote to her sister and Margaret wrote back in secret. They kept in touch for a few months until one of the letters was found somehow, (both Jennifer and Margaret believed Willamina found it and took it to her parents). Margaret was very severely punished and her parents made sure she never had contact with Jennifer again."

"When she married at twenty-six and left home, Margaret wrote to Jennifer explaining everything, but Jennifer had moved house and it was only years later, when a diligent post office worker came across the undelivered letter and decided to trace the recipient, that Jennifer received it. By this time Margaret had died, so again the link was broken."

"No one from the family had anything to do with Jennifer until about twelve years ago. Jennifer became ill and as she had not had any children she became fixated with leaving her wealth to her sister's family. She wrote to them, but none of the family answered – your father was particularly strong in his views about the damage Jennifer had done to his own mother. The punishment Margaret had received for writing to Jennifer had left scars on her body, so it must have been very harsh. Your mother, unbeknown to anyone, took pity on Jennifer and wrote back to apologise for the families behaviour. Jennifer thanked her but said she understood. She told your mother she would like to leave a "little something" for you – but it had to be anonymous, and not knowing quite the size of this "little something", your mother agreed."

"The "trifling amount" turned out to be rather substantial and was what paid for you to do so much travelling, amongst other things. At first your mother tried to give it back, but Jennifer had died and your mother had to deal with Jennifer's rich husband. He insisted it was his wife's wish you have the money, and there was nothing more to say."

"Your grandmother had set up a bank account for you the day you were born and put some money into it every birthday and also at other times during the year. Luckily your father had never bothered to find out how much was in this account, so your mother put your new inheritance in that account with the other money and your father never suspected anything odd."

"Your mother wrote to Jennifer's husband, keeping him informed of how the money was being spent. Even though he insisted he trusted her to use it for you, she told him every detail of your travels and sent him pictures. He treasured these things as a part of Jennifer, and as he got older they became very important to him. When your parents died in the plane crash he contacted Alain and me about paying for the funeral anonymously. We organised it to look as if they had an insurance policy that covered the expenses. He asked us to keep an eye on you and let him know how you were and if you needed anything, which you never did."

"Jennifer's husband's name was Marcel Picard and, as you said, he died recently, a very old man, with no living family left. He left his fortune and business to you. The money is considerable, millions actually, and the business has been running very successfully for years without Marcel's involvement. You can keep it running or sell it for another fortune, whichever you prefer. Alain went to Northern Ireland to meet you and get you to sign the inheritance documents, but he obviously didn't make it and was killed first."

"For years we have come across Willamina and her family trying all sorts of underhand tactics to get their hands on Marcel's fortune, but we never considered they would commit murder to do it. I believe we were wrong."

"I brought a new version of the contract for you to sign, as I believe once it is signed, you will be safe. Once you sign it the money recedes from Willamina's grasp, but until then, if you are killed, Willamina's family may have a legitimate claim, and if they did kill Alain to stop him getting the contract to you, you will be next - to stop you signing."

He handed me the document, and while my brain was in overdrive processing all this information, it did work well enough to make me wary of signing a contract without getting a lawyer of my own to read it.

However, it was in English and could not have been simpler.

"I Amanda Broughton, the undersigned, accept the estate of Marcel Picard in its entirety. There are no debts and no family to claim any or all of this estate. The inheritance comprises the sum of €52,008,719.13 and the business located in Rue Chambal, 57, which included the premises, merchandise, clients and good name. This is valued at €27.500,000. Also part of the estate is the Chateau Picard and adjacent vineyard, value €3,500,000."

I read this and re-read it, trying to ignore the vast figures, and seeing no trick in its simplicity I signed. I had felt frightened and Jacques was right, after signing I did feel relieved, but until Willamina knew the contract was signed, and it was a done deal, I supposed I was still at risk and said so to Jacques.

He agreed and saying he had good contacts in London, we set off for the Metropolitan Police. He must indeed have some clout, for despite having no appointment we were ushered into the commissioner's office nearly straight away. The head of the force listened to us intently and after looking at my photos, issued an arrest warrant for the whole of Willamina's family. He told me that way I would be safe, and if any of the family could prove they were innocent they would be released later on, but in the meantime he suggested we call an immediate press conference to let the world know I was a millionaire.

The police later informed us that they had investigated Willamina's family and believed it was them who had murdered Alain, dumping him near my house in the hope I would be suspected. Someone had also planted the gun in a rockery in my garden; partially concealed but visible enough if you were looking for it. Apparently there was enough evidence for a conviction, but what this was, they refused to discuss, but I suppose I should be grateful to the police for their bungling, as they did not search for suspects early on, believing as they did that it was suicide. If they had the gun may have surfaced in my garden, putting me at the top of their list.

Jacques organised the sale of all the businesses and property, except the house and vineyard. I moved into Marcel's Chateau, where keeping all the staff, I ran the winery – successfully, I might add, along with my new husband, Jacques.

The first year we had an excellent vintage and sat down to toast our success in front of a blazing fire.

"We pulled it off, and we didn't even need your alibi of being on the phone with me at the time of the murder, said Jacques.

We lifted out glasses and toasted our inventive and successful plan that had allowed us to get rid of the true heirs and ensure the estate came to me.

Dark Places

I remember the day I was sent to the orphanage well. People always said I was too young to recall it, but every detail is clear in my mind and every time I think about it, it is like watching a film.

First I was led through long, dark corridors and then a doctor examined me and asked strange questions. I never found out if I answered them well or not, but straight away I was led to a dungeon and locked into a big room.

It was dark and although I could see nothing, I could feel a presence. I called out to whoever it was, asking them to answer, but only heard a strange scraping noise. I called again but this time there was only heavy silence.

I had not seen the room well before the door was closed, and fearful of tripping over something I decided to step back until I was touching the door. That way I could work my way round the walls and try and find my bed or a table and chair.

I took a step back, then another, and another, but still the door was out of reach. I knew I had not walked far into the room and couldn't think why I could not find the door. I held my hands out in front of me and tried walking a bit, but before long my foot shook. I didn't know what made it shake and the thought frightened me. I got down onto the floor on my knees and felt with my hands. There was nothing there, and I do mean nothing. That was why my foot had not felt stable; half of it had been standing over the edge of a hole. I sat down shaken, and after a while, when I felt a bit better, I tried feeling my way again with my hands, but I was surrounded by nothing. The space where I sat was all the area I had – not even enough to lie down.

I was frightened and did not understand anything. Why had I been brought to this orphanage? Both my mother and father were alive, and I had a little brother too, so I wasn't an orphan. Why had my brother not been brought with me? Why had I been locked into this room? How had a hole surrounded me when I had walked over it to get here?

Time passed. I have no way of knowing how much, as with no light it could have been a couple of hours or a few days. At first my body ached terribly from being stuck in the same position but after a while even that passed and I became numb. I was terrified about falling asleep, as I might fall over and tumble down into the void. Every now and again I felt round me with my hands, hoping to find an area I could cross so I could move a bit or lie down, but all that happened was I became convinced the hole was moving towards me and my sitting area was getting smaller and smaller, but I did think this must be caused by fear and not reality.

Every second I was there I felt the presence of another person - an evil aura was keeping me company, but whoever they were they never made a sound or spoke and I came to believe it was my imagination. I did realise the disappearing area where I sat was not a figment of my imagination when it got so small I had to sit as if on a chair with my legs dangling over the edge. I had no way of knowing how deep the fall was, but I remembered a day walking on the mountains, when my parents had still wanted me, there had been a deep hole there too and it had made my voice sound funny. It sounded just like that here too, so I thought it likely the drop was so big I would be killed.

Days passed, until, finally I was standing on one foot only, as there was no space for the other one and even that part was quickly vanishing.

I had expected it to slowly disappear but what happened surprised me for many reasons. Suddenly the remaining area was removed in a rush and I was left in mid-air. I had expected to fall, but that didn't happen.

I waited and waited - for something terrible which never came. Again I have no way of knowing how much time passed, but suddenly I did realise I did not need the ground – the air held my weight and with relief I lay down, suspended in the air, and had a long and deep sleep.

I woke up feeling much better and very angry. I stood up and walked through the air and this time I did find the door. When my hand touched it the door exploded and I was free.

Free to do anything I wanted, and I wanted revenge on everyone responsible for closing me in there – and what Lucifer wants, Lucifer gets.

Hit Song

When I woke up this morning I felt excited and inspired. I just knew I was going to make lots of money today - I don't know how I knew this, but it was a certainty, not an aspiration.

Feeling euphoric I decided the usual muesli and instant coffee was too uninteresting a way to start a day like this - so I had hot buttered croissants and real coffee. Then I sat down with a blank piece of paper and a pen. Within the space of about fifteen minutes I had written a song; music, lyrics, the whole bit. Incredulous, I checked it for errors, but as befitted the day, there were none.

Next I searched the internet for music moguls, found a few quickly and sent off my song. It was now 11.23am. I phoned asking a friend to meet me for lunch and the exhilaration I was feeling must have been noticeable as she asked me more than once if I had been drinking. I hadn't, but a few glasses of wine with lunch and a short shopping spree afterwards did little to calm me down.

Back home I couldn't settle down to doing anything, so lit the fire and sat down with another glass of wine and a good book.

At 4.58pm I received an email offering me the simplest contract I could have imagined; a staggering amount of money for the use of my song with a clause offering me more money if I wrote another nine songs.

I couldn't believe how easy and quick it had all been, but the bottle of champagne sitting in the fridge for months was begging to be opened *right now* in celebration.

Unfortunately the popping of the cork woke me before I had a chance to drink it.

Fireside Reading

One of my favourite pastimes was sitting in front of a blazing fire and reading. I loved books and read different genres in different circumstances; afternoon sofa reading was a learning experience: famous tall ships, exploration and so on; bedtime reading was light fiction and fireside reading was poetry, autobiographies and the like.

On both sides of the fireplace were book lined shelves and I chose the day's book based on my humour of the moment. Fireside reading was a sort of ritual. First I lit the fire and also a few strategically placed incense sticks, then I put on soft background music and sat in a comfy armchair.

One particular day which, at the time, felt no different to any other, I settled to Vivaldi, sandalwood and Michael J Fox's autobiography. I was so engrossed in the tale it was only when I remembered to look up and check if the fire needed stoking that I noticed one book sitting quite a bit further out than the others. It was so far out I worried it might fall, so I got up and pushed it back.

I sat down again, but before I could lower my eyes to Michael, I saw it was still sticking out. I was sure I had pushed it right in, but either I was mistaken or something was making it come out. This time I lifted it right out and checked the space behind. Finding nothing there, I put it back, checking to see if it was in line with the other books on the shelf. It was, so I turned and went back to my armchair. I glanced back before sitting down and sure enough it was out again.

Now that really was odd. As I neared the bookcase the book seemed to leap out and fly straight into my arms. I caught it and it fell open. My eyes fell onto a phrase on the page as if it had been highlighted, (which it hadn't, "I am a relation of yours ", but as I was about to read on a movement caught my eye and I saw another book sliding out by itself.

Weird as it seemed, there could be little doubt that someone, relation or not, was trying to tell me something. My overriding feeling was of curiosity rather than fear, so I replaced the book I was holding and waited a while to see if it came back out or if I had got the entire message from it. The book stayed put so I went on to the next one and again it immediately fell open to a page where a sentence stood out again. "I want to help ".

Not knowing how many messages would come my way I went to get a pen and paper to jot them down. There were seven in total and I doubt I would have remembered that many word for word. I wrote them down separately in the order they had been shown to me but I wasn't sure if they were coming in the correct order or needed to be mixed, interpreted or what.

This is what I got:
"I am a relation of yours"
"I want to help"
"find the treasure"
"it has been hidden too long"
"look under a rock"
"the secret is"
"in the garden"

These caused me a few dilemmas. Was it, "I want to help find the treasure" or "I want to help." "Find the treasure"?

Why were the first messages perfectly clear and complete but the last two or three looked like a riddle? And the phrase, "the secret is"; was this incomplete or was it "the secret is in the garden"? I had checked the book where "the secret is" came from but even if a word was missing it still didn't make sense as the next word in the book was "mine", followed by a full stop.

Then there was the totally inexplicable part of "looking under a rock" and "in the garden". This made it sound as if something was hidden in the garden under a rock. Simple enough in theory, but I had made a few rock gardens, so there were loads of rocks to move and look under, but this only made it a question of time and effort, and if I looked under them all, sooner or later I would find it – but, and this was a big but, I had bought a newly built house, so there was no connection with my rocks to any of my relations, so this meant I must be missing something.

I sat looking at the phrases, arranging and re-arranging them for ages but got no further on.

It was winter and by the time I stopped analysing this conundrum it was dark outside, so there was little I could do at that point anyway.

I went to make dinner and while I was eating it I thought some more, but short of digging up more or less all my garden I couldn't figure out what to do. Also there was a part of me that was starting to doubt the advisability of excavating my carefully placed flowers on the basis of a few books that moved. And yet, I couldn't stop thinking about it.

58

After dinner I went back into the lounge, intending to watch television and saw another book sitting on the edge of the bookcase. This one opened at, "time is running out".

Great! Now I was being threatened by books. This was getting out of hand, so I turned on the television and tried to concentrate on a murder mystery, but yet another out of place book was driving me mad with curiosity.

Ignoring it was not working, so I managed to hold off until the ads and then went to see what new clue was awaiting me. It was another threat of sorts, "do something quickly". Frustrated I virtually yelled, "It's dark. I can't do anything until daylight."

A book popped out.

"Ah", so I could communicate with them, that certainly had not occurred to me before and made a huge difference.

"No!"

"No what? No, don't wait, go outside in the dark and cold to look under rocks?" I questioned, putting the book back.

Another book, another "no".

"All right." I need to try again, I thought, and this time with a clear question - "Is this treasure outside under a rock?"

"No."

More in frustration than anything else I sighed, "Well it can't be inside under a rock".

"Yes."

"But there are no rocks in the house."

"Yes, there are."

That stopped me. It meant I had to look at this differently, so I set off on a room to room search for a "rock".

Actually there were a few, if you take the term loosely. I had a few lumps of crystal, which were a type of rock. There were pebbles in the fish tank – small rocks - a polished stone paperweight and two carved stone statues which had once been rocks. I gathered them all and assembled them in the lounge. Before I could ask I got a "no", but I noticed "Rock Hudson's Autobiography" was protruding slightly. Rock!

Under "Rock" was the first edition of "The Secret Garden" that had been in my family for ages. That had to be it!

I lifted out the old book and a piece of paper fell out. This was a book I had always intended to read but had never got around to, which was why I had not known there was anything inside.

The paper was a faded hand written list:
Indian
French Man's Woman
Musical Military

Oblivious to the late hour I tried to make sense of these, the television long abandoned and forgotten. I automatically assumed the names on the list were books, so they only needed deciphering as obviously this was some sort of code. If they were books and I had guessed right, I knew why the hurry and it all made sense.

I checked with the book shelves before opening the packet I had carefully wrapped and left on the table earlier that day, and got confirmation I was right.

I had inherited a large and varied collection of books and one was "The Pilgrim's Progress" in Cree Indian. At first I had kept this as a fascination but soon felt this was a waste having it as I could not read or enjoy it and had recently advertised it on the internet. The book had sold quickly and was currently sitting all wrapped and ready for the courier to collect first thing tomorrow morning.

This was the only "Indian" book I had, so I unwrapped it and sure enough an envelope fluttered out. I carefully checked the book in case anymore notes were hidden, but finding nothing I wrapped it up again, ready for collection.

Strange it hadn't fallen out before now, either the times I had looked through the book or while wrapping it earlier that day, but on the occasions I had picked it up I had not opened all the pages and the envelope had been wedged against the spine, so that was probably why I had overlooked it, along with the fact I had not been looking for hidden messages. I was dying to open it, but building suspense by finding them all first and then opening them all in one go seemed more exciting.

"French Man's Woman" must be French Lieutenant's Woman, although at first I couldn't find the book and began to wonder if I did have it, (I didn't remember ever seeing it). It turned up in the bottom left corner and my search was rewarded with another envelope.

Just the last one to go. Musical Military sounded like the history of the drum, parades or something similar, and I knew my grandfather had enjoyed that genre, but there were only two possible ones and they held nothing.

I thought and searched until not long before three o'clock and finding nothing I felt it time to give up. It wasn't there. I had already established a few hours ago the books could not tell me what book to search for, but I asked them if they could confirm it was a book I owned and had in my house, which they did. I did get a "bedroom" hint which was useful as I had totally forgotten about the small bookcase of light reading I kept for bed.

I went upstairs and immediately saw "The Trumpet Major" – obvious when you know the answer. Opening it I got the final envelope wedged between pages 8 and 9. I returned to the fire and before opening the three mysterious missives asked if this was all there were. It was, so I thanked the books for helping me, feeling slightly foolish I must admit, and sat down.

The contents were incredible. They were three signed notes or letters to three different members of my family and all from famous names. A famous composer wrote, "When I wrote – a small musical score was drawn - I was thinking of you. You will hear this music often and always know what you meant to me. It will also be exciting that you and I will be the only two people in the whole world to know the secret of this music my darling." (I tried playing it later on the piano and it was a very well-known masterpiece of classical music.)

A celebrated writer said, "Your incredible beauty sustains me when I have my bad heads, and Alice dear, you are so much in my thoughts you also become part of my hallucinations during the bad heads. I wrote a book about it and called the main character by your name."

Britain's best known author, (famous for writing about penury, a subject he well knew), penned, "Sir, your kindness and generosity to me when I was in harder times has not been forgotten. The enclosed locket, (and he described it), was my mother's and is for your beautiful daughter with my eternal gratitude and thanks."

Wow! I was wearing that very locket. I thought about it for a few days and decided to sell the first two letters, frankly as I needed the money, but I would keep the one detailing how the locket had come into my family.

The letters were judged genuine and fetched considerable sums, leaving me debt free and even quite wealthy.

The books never spoke to me again, even when I questioned them about the one thing I didn't understand – I had just read the Trumpet Major, finishing it the night before the discovery of the envelopes.

Old Love

There I was in the middle of the supermarket, trolley loaded with totally unnecessary essentials, when I heard it. Our song. Why do good times have to turn sad, and why do they always come back to haunt you at the most inconvenient times? As I paused, ostensibly to make the difficult choice between processed and garden peas, it all came back...

The rose covered cottage where lazy afternoons were spent making wonderful love. Horses were grazing in the sun outside the window, patiently waiting in case we wanted to go for a ride, while that song played over and over on our new machine. Actually, it wasn't playing only our song, merely once every now and again; it just seemed to be all we heard. Mark sang along, but only to the words about love and always looking at me. We had everything in common, shared so much, and both wanted to get married – eventually, but were content for now to leave things as they were.

What went wrong? We were so much in love until that dreadful holiday. The fights over nothing, either one or both of us in tears, or a terrible rage, and yet, neither able to let the other go.

Maybe if we hadn't gone on a cruise, but rather an ordinary holiday, then I could have changed rooms or even hotels – maybe then there would have been less resentment and we could have worked it out. As it was, we were stuck with each other, with little time to escape and that mad resentment built up to amazing levels, until there was no going back.

We had chosen the "50th anniversary, once only, cruise of a lifetime. Six weeks of travelling in luxury from one exotic place to another." The only luxury we were aware of was the large bed, which allowed us to balance on our respective edges, with only a minimum risk of falling out.

There were wonderful trips ashore for sightseeing and shopping, but neither of us able to appreciate much of what we saw, although we did manage to accumulate a lot of silly mementoes. We bartered and spent the last of our money, the way you always feel compelled to do on holiday, as if it is a great sin to actually take some home. We were both too miserable to make friends, so that left us with only each other and our bitterness. I don't think either of us could really say how or why the fighting started, but it did and both of us said things the other could neither forgive nor forget – so it went on, and on.

Five weeks into the journey from hell was Egypt. This was the main reason we had chosen this cruise, both of us wishing to fulfil a dream to visit this place that was so full of fascinating history. By silent, mutual accord, a temporary truce was called and we left the ship in reasonably good moods to do all the tourist things - the pyramids, the pharaoh's tombs, even Tutankhamun's, rounding off with a trip up, (or was it down), the Nile. This left about four o'clock, lasted two hours, and was commonly called the 'Sundowner Cruise'. Accordingly we were given sun downers which, added to the capacious amounts of wine we had drunk with lunch, put us in a festive mood, better able to appreciate the magnificent sunset. There was a bright orange sky, no sun, just everything aglow with orange light. This, our guide assured us, was a real treat to be cherished, and cherish it we did by putting our arms round each other.

Dinner that night was in a cave, which I think was supposed to represent a tomb. The food was lovely, and there was more wine to make us feel mellow, providing we didn't fall over first. We left, arm in arm, to go for a walk. The closeness was not due to the wine; perhaps it was the magic that was Egypt, or maybe we had both managed to grow up. Whatever the reason, it lasted until we were in our cabin and then things managed to get worse than ever, although I hadn't thought that possible.

Only one stop left, and then we would be on our way home. One step nearer to never seeing each other again. I don't know which was worse; this time spent hurting each other or never seeing him again?

The flight home was uneventful and passed in a flash, just as the time since Egypt had. We had certainly got the cruise of a lifetime. One I was never to forget. I wonder did Mark?

Oh dear, I'm going to cry. Not here - I mustn't cry here in the supermarket. I won't. I won't cry. Yes, I will, I am having trouble seeing, and things are already blurred. I'll leave the trolley, pretending I am just going up the next aisle to get something else and slip quietly out.

At last, alone in the car. Still, I mustn't cry loudly, someone might hear and come over to see what is wrong, and I am too old to be crying like this for lost love, even one that hurts so very much. I can't seem to stop. The tears just keep coming and my tissues are in the trolley in the supermarket. Oh Mark, I love you so much and I miss you. Why can't we be together? I should have been Mrs Turney. What went wrong?

"Darling, wake up! I have brought you breakfast in bed, my beautiful bride. What happened? Your pillows are soaking."

64

"I know, I had a nightmare dear," as I struggle to sit up without spilling the coffee. "This is lovely. Do I get this every morning or is this morning special?" I asked, smiling at the dear man.

"Is this morning special she asks! This is your first morning as my wife, Mrs Clarke. Of course it is special, and tomorrow it is your turn to get up. This marriage is a democracy."

"Yes Peter, of course," I replied, trying to leave the dream behind.

"And I have a surprise for you before we leave on our honeymoon. Do you recall me talking about my best friend in university?"

"Oliver?"

"Yes, although that isn't his real name of course, but anyway he is downstairs as he wanted to meet you and wish us luck. You remember yesterday was his father's funeral so he couldn't come to the wedding?"

"How nice of him. I have heard so much about him I feel I already know him and can't wait to meet him. What is his real name?"

"Well, he loved Dickens at school, (he was the only one in the whole school), and we used to tease him about it, and as his surname was so similar to 'twist' we always called him Oliver but his name is Mark Turney."

In the News

The Monday drudge arrived and I collected the paper from the front mat to read while I ate my cornflakes, as usual. Unsurprisingly, the front page was full of sensational stories; today was about a train wreck with photos of wreckage strewn all around and the title "Mayhem in Middle". I didn't know what you were supposed to deduce from that, but I suppose whoever wrote it thought it clever for some reason.

I knew I would hear about it on the news that evening, and as time was tight, I turned straight to the money pages – (as a financial advisor I needed to keep up to date with what was worth what), to accompany a strong cup of coffee.

The day did not go as planned; it didn't even go well, although that was an understatement. I had taken the train to meet an important client, believing it to be the quickest way to travel to my destination and so avoiding traffic jams, rush hour and other long and frustrating holdups. Unfortunately some idiot had tried to drive his car across a level crossing when the barriers were down and had got stuck. He then panicked, abandoned his car, and ran for safety long before the train arrived. Luckily the car had been on a straight stretch of track and the train driver had had time to brake before impact, thus saving many lives, including mine. The train had run into the car and gone off the rails, but we were going so slowly when we hit, the train more or less slid off the rails and gently turned onto its side.

It was hours before I got home, with doctors examining me, (only a few bruises and small cuts from broken glass), police asking questions, and finally waiting for a bus to take us all back to where we had started from. All I wanted on opening my front door was a strong glass of whiskey, or two, and to collapse into bed.

Everyone on the train had been bashed about a bit, some were hit by flying glass and a few had broken bones, but nothing was as serious as it could, or should have been, although that did not make any difference to the emotional effect of seeing people flung about and of not knowing where you were going to end up, hence my recourse to glasses of oblivion.

Tuesday morning dawned with some new aches and pains, but I had expected that. Once again I got the paper while coffee was brewing, and opening it saw the headline was about bank robbers - "Gun-less Armed Robbery", no less, but with little time I didn't bother reading it and went straight to the money pages. I left for work intending to peruse the paper fully that evening to see if the crash was mentioned, but fate had other ideas.

After a good strong coffee to set me up for the day, I left for work. Tuesday was quiet in the financial offices where I worked and by lunchtime I was done. I had been meaning to go to the bank for ages, a chore I hated, and today was a good time to get that over with. As I was standing in the queue three masked men came in, one of them armed. They did the usual "Nobody move and you won't get hurt routine", and headed for the cashiers. The one with the gun went to the head of my queue and told the teller to hand over all the money. The cashier did, setting it on the counter as he would for any client, and the robber was so absorbed in filling his bag – one hand holding it open, the other putting rolls of bank notes in - he set the gun on the counter! I tapped the only person in front of me in the queue and indicating what I wanted, got her to step quietly aside. Then I managed to pick up the gun and convince the robber to surrender, by holding it to his temple. It really was as easy as that, and once the other masked men saw what had happened, they fled. (I should add that I had done a stint in the army and knew how to use a weapon, I wasn't just a passerby who thought he was Rambo.) The police came along with the inevitable news reporters and I was told my heroics would be tomorrow's front page news, (with what headline remained to be seen).

An editor from the same paper I read every day was waiting to talk to me on my front door step. Apparently it was my civic duty to give him an interview which would be published as "an insider's view of the robbery." I told him I had already talked to his reporter, but he said that was for the front page news story and this was "human interest" on page seven, (at least it wasn't page three!) He accepted a whiskey as I answered his questions, and yet again dinner was liquid, but this time I got an early night.

I won't say Wednesday morning dawned bright and fine, but it did dawn. I woke up as the alarm rang and with more aches and pains, which I hadn't expected. This made getting ready for work take longer than normal and I had little time for the paper, but today I intended to read the front page first - after all I would be on it.

It wasn't there! I scanned the rest of the paper quickly but could find nothing about my heroics, only a few articles on con men, scams, hustles and people selling Tower Bridge or Buckingham Palace or something else silly. Page seven also had no mention of the robbery, so money markets were again perused with coffee, before a dash to work.

What a week so far and it had only just started. I hoped today would be the normal humdrum accountancy work of checking figures and doing sums, followed by a proper dinner and some television.

Work that day was filled with what was, unfortunately, becoming normal - all sorts of illegal requests from clients, carefully couched in ambiguous terms. I don't know why people think it is fine to ask a financial advisor how to launder money or evade tax, when the same people would believe it madness to ask a policeman the best way to rob a bank!

One of these requests stood out, not for the actual request, but rather the tirade that followed my careful refusal. Somewhere in there, was the accusation that a person in my position had helped the last time and therefore I could too, and it sounded very much as if this 'helpful' person were with this firm.

I only dealt with our top clients, all extremely wealthy, and the firm's policy was not to overload me with work so I could always be available to do these moneyed men's bidding. This worked well for everyone and often left me with spare time to brush up on current trends, potential new markets and anything else worth researching, or simply to leave early, thereby making up for frequent obligatory business dinners and late nights. I used the time that day to go over that particular client's history with our firm - just to see.

He had come to me about eighteen months previously, after his last advisor Mr. McArthur, one of the partners and a founder member of the firm, had retired. A man of impeccable reputation and 'a genius of the financial world', it really didn't seem likely he had done any dirty deals – but, as it seemed probable someone had, that was as good a place to start as any. I wasn't investigating the partner; after all he was independently wealthy and had no need for this sort of underhand dealing, never mind his squeaky clean image, but I did think it possible he had been away or ill and another accountant had stepped in for a short period.

Four or five hours later I had it. It wasn't even hidden, but I supposed he thought no one would check, and they wouldn't have if the client had not let it slip out in the heat of the moment. I had checked and checked again, then looked for other explanations and finally had phoned the police. It was late by then and everyone else had gone home. I had tried to contact my boss but, as luck would have it, he was not at home and his mobile was switched off.

The police arrived along with their own expert and it didn't take him long to concur with my findings. There was no doubt - it was all there in black and white - and it was a massive swindle of millions of pounds. They set off there and then to

68

arrest Mr. McArthur and all the others involved - which apparently included my boss because they thought he must have known. (It turned out later he hadn't, but the men who were involved went to jail for quite a few years.)

That day turned out to be the longest yet and it was 5.30am before I got home, after helping the police with their enquiries, and no, that is not a euphemism for being arrested. They wanted to know how things worked in the firm and asked me to go through other ledgers with their financial expert.

I had a large mug of coffee and went to bed, remembering to switch off the alarm clock. There would be no work the next day as the police had sealed off our offices, so I could sleep late and recover from the ordeals that had plagued me recently.

I woke just after lunchtime and was hungry, but was too exhausted after everything that had gone on that week to make food, so I threw a tracksuit on over my pyjamas and bought a ready meal in the small shop on the corner. It would be ready after spending three minutes in the microwave, the packet informed me. I used that time to remove the tracksuit and make coffee, then, still drained, I took my feast back to bed.

Once finished I fell asleep almost immediately, only to wake up soon after sweating and with terrible stomach pain. As things got worse I called the doctor who said he would send an ambulance, and enquired if the door was locked. It was of course, but I struggled to it and remedied this before dragging myself into the bathroom.

Nothing more registered until I woke in a hospital bed the next day to see my worried girlfriend sitting beside me. Apparently it had been touch and go when she had got a call on her mobile, and not knowing she was in France on business, the caller suggested she make haste to the hospital.

As the whole story emerged it sounded more like a film than my real life for the past couple of days.

A policeman had arrived at my house to ask me some more questions about the swindle just as ambulance men were carrying me out, and the police were worried this was not simply food poisoning but one of the money launderers trying to make sure I was not available to testify. They had called my girlfriend and posted a guard outside my door - but it turned out to be normal food poisoning, and the hospital was inundated with similar cases. (When I say normal, I mean not poisoning aimed at me. The food had been deliberately poisoned by terrorists to rail against the food producing company setting up in their South American country without paying the due 'protection' to said terrorists.)

I was kept in hospital a few days for observation, and having nothing to do I read the papers from cover to cover, but there was little of interest. Catching me with the paper one day the sister commented on this lack of news, adding that for four days there had been so many dramatic events it seemed odd to see nothing drastic on the front page to shock readers. Feigning things to do, and therefore lack of interest, she said, with a blush, that I had become quite a celebrity with my heroic deeds and miraculous escape from the train crash.

It *had* been quite a week and I had been so busy lurching from one disaster to another I really hadn't had time to reflect on my misfortunes. Sister was saying something else that sounded wrong too, although I hadn't been paying enough attention to pinpoint what. Hairs on the back of my neck standing up, I asked her to repeat what she had said.

She did and I knew what wasn't right. The days were off by one. They hadn't happened when she said. She was talking about the con men I was responsible for catching on Tuesday, but it had happened on Wednesday. She even said she had read about it on Wednesday. Alarm bells were ringing.

I asked her if she had read about the train crash too and when she confirmed that had been in Tuesday's paper I tried in vain to remember this week's front page news. It was no good; I hadn't read the articles, didn't know the details and could not remember what news had been plastered over the page on which day, so I asked if there were old papers in the hospital. There weren't, so I sent Leila, (my girlfriend), on a quest to root out that week's newspapers, without telling her why – after all it did sound a bit farfetched. She came back a bit later with a bundle and together we looked at the headlines. They corresponded with sister's dates; one day after the actual event had taken place – just as I had thought.

These papers were the large format, and the one delivered to my home was the smaller version. I didn't know whether they were both identical or if the smaller one was a different version, however unlikely this seemed. Not wishing to alarm Leila I said nothing about my fears as she had to return to Paris for three more days to finish her job, so I wished her a speedy return and she wished me no more dramatic events, and we said goodbye.

I couldn't wait to read all that week's small versions and that meant going home to see if I could find mine - I kept them in a box and used them for lighting the fire, but if memory served I hasn't lit it for a few days so they should all be there.

Both sizes should be the same, but maybe they weren't and one was an early edition. Thinking back, how I came to have the smaller paper was a bit strange - there had been a knock at the door on Sunday morning and a man who looked familiar had offered to deliver my normal paper in a smaller, more manageable size, free of charge for six months, after which I would pay the usual price. It had seemed like a good deal and I had accepted, although now I did wonder why he worked on a Sunday and why it was free for so long.

When I finally got home I went straight to my newspaper pile and picked up the top bundle.
I rummaged through until I got all that week's together. I was lucky and they were all there. It wasn't hard to find them, as I had changed supplier only the day before this had all started and the new papers were the only ones that shape, and consequently stood out from the large muddle that was my fire stack under the stairs.

I laid them on the table, careful not to open any until I was ready, and once Monday, Tuesday, Wednesday and Thursday were in order I took a deep breath and started. It was all there in black and white, just as incriminating and damming as the con men's deeds had been.

Each morning's headlines had explained in detail what was to happen to me that day. I was even mentioned by name in them all. I dropped into a chair. Strange how shocked you can be by finding something you are looking for.

I read them all many times then phoned the police. Two officers arrived quickly, probably alerted to something hysterical in my voice. Knowing I was going to sound a bit odd I asked what day I had called them about the swindle in my firm. They confirmed it was Wednesday with a note of worry in their voice, and I handed them the paper, pointing to the relevant story. They read it and shrugged before handing the paper back. I shook my head and told them to read the date on the paper. They did. The older one registered nothing, but the other went white and dropped into a chair, just as I had. We looked at each other, but the more experienced officer was having none of our flights of fantasy and said it was probably a misprint. I handed him the larger version of that day's paper with the correct date and a different headline and he did look slightly perplexed, but not much. I then got them to examine Monday's, Tuesday's and Thursday's and when they had finished all three of us were sitting numb.

The younger policeman got up to make tea and this returned some semblance of normality to the situation. I explained about the man on Sunday offering the smaller version and as I was coming to the end of that tale the kettle boiled and the doorbell rang in sync. The young detective went to answer it and came back saying it was my paper provider who called to let me know they could no longer deliver my small format paper, so I would have to go back to the old version. He had been very quick thinking and had answered the door with his phone turned to camera and had a picture of the 'paper boy'.

As he showed us the photo I realized why the man had looked recognizable, (I had thought he was from a newsagent's or other shop I frequented), but as we looked at the phone we were looking at an image of the famous media mogul, Robert someone or other, (none of us could remember the surname), who apparently fell off his boat in such a wave of controversy.

The Flyer

We had just bought a new house in an area far from where we had lived for the last ten years. The company my husband worked for had a branch and headquarters in that area, and he had been given a promotion and transferred to manage the branch there. We had no choice in this move, not if Tom wanted to keep his job, but with no children, unless you count two dogs and one cat, the move was really quite welcome and exciting. We had visited the area while there to choose our new home, and really liked it, so we were both looking forward to the new start. The house itself was a dream, and as it was about twenty minutes out of the town, it cost less than the more accessible ones, and we were able to buy a bigger house than we believed we could afford. This house was really stretching our budget, but it was so perfect we both felt it was worth giving up the odd dinner in a restaurant for a while if that helped us achieve this dream home.

Everything was packed and our old house sold and emptied, so we stayed at a friend's house for the last ten days until our new home was ready.

It was all going so well I started to get worried. When things all fall into place nicely there is usually a great big anvil in the sky waiting for you to walk under it. We did!

My husband's work place changed the goal posts at the last minute, (well two days before we moved), and he was "asked" to stay an extra six weeks before he could leave without any consequences. It was only a request, but couched in such terms we were in no doubt his whole future depended on him agreeing. Now this sort of blackmail, for that is what it is, really annoyed us and is not something we wanted to give in to; but, having no alternative, he stayed to "help them out" and I went on alone.

We were both angry at this treatment and Tom resolved to find a job with a different firm and leave this one as soon as possible, but until then real life demanded we have an income, and Tom's wage was our only one. I had left my job a couple of months earlier so I had time to pack up, and we had both agreed I should set up the house and get everything just right before looking for another, so I was currently unemployed.

I arrived that first day and felt sad at Tom's absence, angry at the company, and disappointed that our "wonderful new life" had started in such a bitter way. Tom had to work overtime during this period, so Sundays were his only time off and the distance was too great for him to visit for a day. It seemed a long time to be apart, especially with no friends nearby. There were practical problems too and I had yet to figure out how to move the big pieces of furniture by myself. I had no idea where Tom would want his stuff, (neither did he until he saw the room set up) – all sorts of inconveniences plagued me, but I knew I would have to put them out of my mind and get on with sorting out our new lives.

I was working in the house the first day I got the keys, trying valiantly to clean the rooms before our furniture arrived and the clutter made things more difficult, when there was a knock at the door.

Reluctantly I went to answer, partly afraid it was the furniture arriving early, (that would be a first), but fearing it was a new neighbour come to say hello. I didn't want to stop and chat but I could hardly say, "Go away I don't want to talk now", to a stranger coming with the best of intentions.

Outside was a lady in gardening clothes with a broom, sponge and cloth in her hand. "Hello, I'm Amy and I thought you were probably cleaning while the house was empty so I came to give you a hand. We can get to know each other when the work is done. I will bring round a bottle of wine later and we can chat then. Where do you want me to start?"

"Wow! I'm Suzy and thank you that all sounds perfect."

She proceeded to take squashed sandwiches and two plastic cups out of her pocket and throw them onto the counter while declaring "Lunch". Then she turned awaiting instructions.

Together we got everywhere done in time and once the furniture arrived we got the bed in place, and made, and even a few kitchen boxes unpacked so I could live there that night without too much discomfort. After that she had dragged me to her house about 50 metres away, gave me a huge drink, introduced her husband and fed me.

That was the beginning of a wonderful friendship. Amy was bubbly and great fun, but a serious worker too. She really got things done, but made doing them fun for anyone involved. It was one of those friendships where she always seemed to be helping me and I never got the chance of paying her back. She was organised and needed nothing and she didn't ask for anything either... until one day a few months after we had settled in.

It was late afternoon when she came over and I knew something strange was going on. She was quieter and fidgeted and would not get to the point, all of which were very unlike her. Eventually I dragged it out of her. She loved bingo.

I was dumbfounded – not just because she liked bingo, but because this declaration seemed to be a big deal and it shouldn't have caused this level of anxiety. Then the whole story came out – there was bingo that night in the town next to ours and she wanted to go, but not alone. Would I go too?

I said I would, although I was not a bingo fan, but told her I didn't know anything about it so I would just watch.

No, that was no good, I had to play too. OK, if that was something I could do for her I would willingly play, provided she explained a bit about how to do it.

Everything settled we arranged to meet at 7.00pm to have a glass of wine first, but just as she was leaving she asked me not to tell Tom. Before I could question the reason for this secrecy, she had disappeared.

Now Tom and I didn't have secrets, so I told him where I was going, but added that he was not supposed to know and from that I deduced Harry, (Amy's husband), didn't know either. It felt a bit like we were going to rob a bank with all the subterfuge, but as our mission was totally legal, we went along. Tom and I did feel it likely someone who knew Amy would see her and say something, but it wouldn't be us.

Amy explained how the game was played in the car, but said not to worry as she would keep an eye on my cards.

"Cards plural," I thought. If I was not mistaken she had said we bought "a" card, but maybe you got two. I just hoped we weren't going to stay for many games as Amy had said they usually last over an hour. As I was calculating how many games we could play and still be home around midnight, (work the next day, for I now had a job), we arrived.

I had always thought bingo was played in cold draughty church halls with ladies with blue rinses, rollers and slippers, but this was the conference room of a hotel – and it was full of well dressed women our age and even younger.

Amy directed me to sit down while she got our cards, she insisted it was her treat and she would pay. I waited wondering how much a card cost and listened to a conversation behind me as two ladies agreed that "only £10 was great value". I hadn't heard what was such good value but couldn't believe they were talking about bingo cards which I thought were probably £1 or maybe even £2.

Amy returned with a huge pile of cards and started laying them out on our two spaces. All the area covered, she layered other cards on top, and then more until each pile had four layers.

"You have to be quick looking at the layers underneath, and don't miss any" she shrieked in a frenzy. I was speechless at the quantity she had bought, and keeping track of all the cards seemed impossible, but I had no chance to say anything. The game started and I did my best, but Amy dived from one pile to the next as if her life depended on it and soon the cards were a bit muddled. The whole time Amy was screaming, "Did you mark number 2? You didn't mark that card. Are you sure you looked properly."

Her voice was getting more and more high pitched, and her movements were becoming jerky and rushed. I was starting to get worried, but I couldn't figure out what I could do about it, as my few attempts at suggesting she calm down had brought forth a tirade of hatred.

When a lady called, 'Bingo', Amy stood up and ripped all her cards to shreds, hurling them onto the ground. This mad person was not the Amy I had come to know in the last five months.

Another game and another pile of cards - bigger than the first. By now she had taken over the table next to ours, when the players there left, and I do think it was Amy's behaviour that made them walk out. (I wished I could too.) Many of the other players were looking at her, some in shock, some with pity and some knowingly. I wanted to ask the knowing ones what they knew, but the game started again. It too ended with another player winning and Amy creating a more worrying scene.

The last game of the evening started, and this time I had got up to buy one card for myself. Partly to give me something to do, as Amy had totally taken over all the other cards on each of the three tables, and partly from curiosity to see how much the cards cost - £20! So the conversation I had overheard was not about bingo cards as these were much more expensive, and to think I thought £2 was dear.

I reckoned Amy had spent thousands of pounds in one evening, somewhere around the £4,000 mark if my calculations were correct, and she was definitely not enjoying it either. This was no "game" for her. It was something serious and the panic and hysterical way she behaved indicated a problem of frightening proportions.

The game progressed and all I wanted was to get Amy home, but I had been so intent on watching her I hadn't paid attention to my own card properly, marking off numbers without looking at the lines, and I suddenly realised I had won, (beginner's luck does exist). I couldn't shout bingo – Amy might kill me the way she was behaving, but I had an idea. I messed with her cards and held mine up triumphantly saying, "Amy you have won. Look!"

She didn't look, but snatched the card, scratching me with her nail in the process, and yelled "BINGO! I won! I won!"

Satisfied it had been a great evening because she had won, we sped our way triumphantly home, and the atmosphere in the car was not as bad as I had dreaded.

Sitting with a cup of coffee and telling Tom about the evening, he said she sounded frightening – as if she were possessed. We had figured out that she was a compulsive gambler and reckoned maybe they did all feel "possessed".

"But with bingo?" I asked.

"Gambling is gambling", Tom replied, adding "it often doesn't matter what they gamble on."

I could not see Amy in the same light after that and was worried she would ask me to go with her again, because I certainly was not going to go.

I needn't have worried; for reasons known only to her, she didn't see me the same way either after that night and barely spoke to me, although Tom and Harry still met for drinks after work. Harry and Amy's house went up for sale soon after that dreadful evening, and sold quickly. On one of their last nights there Tom and Harry went out for a drink. When Tom came home, sober, he said Harry had had too much to drink and had "talked too much."

It had been a very interesting conversation and shows that not only does beginner's luck exist, but also "just desserts".

Going back to Tom's job – he worked for a large company with headquarters in this town and many branches all over the country. Tom worked in one of the branches and had never met the general manager, let alone the owner. Actually, no one in the company seemed to know the name of the owner as it was one of those "holding company" type arrangements and all very secretive.

At the time we were moving house apparently "word had come down from above", (an expression many frustrated businessmen use to avoid saying 'I was ordered to'), that even though Tom's leaving date had been fixed by the company and everything was arranged, he had to stay on another six weeks or his place in the other branch position would be filled by someone else. Basically stay or get out – blackmail as I had said. Now, as I also said, we didn't like this, but the move had been totally dependent on Tom's job and without it we couldn't meet the mortgage repayments on our home, so he stayed.

Once he had moved to our new house, Tom did start looking for another job, as he felt his treatment by the company was unfair and unpleasant, but as yet had only possibilities and no firm offers. He liked his job and colleagues, and if it hadn't been for "Mr Owner" issuing that blackmail note, he would gladly have stayed where he was.

During the drinking session Harry had said he owned a company, (we had been told he did "something" in the City but details had not been forthcoming), and his wife had a gambling problem. To pay his wife's debts and try and save his company he had to sell the house and move in with her parents. The house would "buy him time" to try and sort out something else. Amy had gambled away all their money, sold her jewellery, used the house as collateral and run up debts as well. Harry went on to explain to Tom that this was not the first time. It had happened twelve years ago, but they were just getting back on track financially, when this happened and she had done it again.

Harry said they had moved far from temptation to avoid such an occurrence, and he had done everything possible to keep Amy away from any betting place. They had even moved house a couple of times when a betting shop had been opened in the town near them and he had thought they were safe there.

When people started contacting him about the debts about a week ago he had confronted her and the whole sordid tale had come out. She had gone to bingo one evening and won. Amy had told him I had asked her to go with me, but he assured Tom he knew it was the other way round and he didn't blame me, as I could not have known. It was that win that had fuelled the fire and supposed subsequent shopping trips had really been to bet on other things anywhere she could find. She had gambled online, using the company name to get good credit, and the debts were enormous. Harry thought he may lose the business, although he still hoped to save it somehow.

At first he hadn't known how Amy knew about the damned bingo in the next town, but he had found a leaflet for it in her bag – one of those flyers you get on your car windscreen, and Amy insisted it had been put on her windscreen in their own drive by someone who wished her ill. Naturally Harry didn't believe her, and where it had come from seemed unimportant – it was the damage it had done to his company that worried him most.

At this point he admitted he owned the company Tom worked for. He insisted the only reason he hadn't mentioned it before was because he didn't want Tom to feel bad about having social contact with his boss. Tom assured him pointedly that there were a few things that would upset him, but social contact with his boss was not one of them.

Harry was so wrapped up in his own problems, and they were rather large, he didn't ask what would cause Tom to feel upset, luckily, as that was not the moment to explain.

That flyer and Amy's subsequent win were all it took to set her on the path of destroying her and her husband's life and their company.

Tom and I looked at each other with grins. "I wonder who could have put that flyer on her car?" Tom asked the rhetorical question. "Lucky Harry did not think it important to find out where it came from."

I smiled. "I believe the term is 'Bingo!'"

Freedom in Mind

Freedom is an odd word. I didn't use to think so but now I know it to be true. I used to hate the expression 'freedom is a relative term' and I still do. There is nothing relative about freedom - you either have it or you don't. I don't; but anyone you ask, including my ex-wife, would tell you differently.

I will tell you my story from the beginning and let you judge whether or not I am free for yourself.

Up to that day each day felt like all the others. I was not adventurous, so days tended to be similar, through choice, and my life was predictable – just the way I liked it. One morning, on 3rd March, I woke as usual and made instant coffee the same way I always did, but this particular morning it tasted funny. At the time I didn't think anything of it and set off for work blithely unaware of what lay ahead. Everything else that day was normal – until, on the way home, I stopped at the supermarket and bought fresh pasteurised milk. Now for many people this is normal, but I have hated the taste since I was very young and always used skimmed for everything.

I couldn't work out what had made me buy it, but even more worrying was the insatiable desire to have a bowl of cornflakes and pour lots of the dreaded milk in. I fought against it, but, that is what I had for dinner, and spent my subsequent waking hours trying figure out what was happening. It was my brother Ted who liked milk, not me. Why was the 'need' for this milk so strong I was unable to fight it? And why did it suddenly taste good?

Thinking of Ted just disturbed me more. This was territory I hadn't explored for years. Not since he had left the country and gone to live dear knows where, after running up huge debts in our parents' names as well as actually stealing money from their bank by forging their signature on documents and cheques. They did not prosecute, but made it clear he was not welcome anymore. I think secretly mum and dad forgave him after time passed and hoped he would show up one day, but they died in a car crash without that happening. As far as I knew he didn't even know they had passed away as I had no way to inform him. Most of his friends were also my friends and they too had heard nothing from him since he left. He had also stolen money from the place he worked, and had asked colleagues for loans he never paid back. My parents had asked all the people concerned to let them pay back the large amounts of money and not to prosecute, and without exception they had agreed to do this, so no charges were brought.

Returning to that evening - I eventually went to bed and slept well. Next morning I had more cornflakes and fresh milk, this time I didn't bother fighting this urge too much, and set off for work. As I walked into the area in the building where my office was, my secretary looked at me strangely as she said good morning. In the privacy of my own office I checked all my buttons and zips were closed and my tie straight, and finding nothing amiss dismissed her odd glance as I got down to some demanding work for a client. I worked all morning without interruption and set off happily to meet John, an old friend who I only saw occasionally, for lunch.

I arrived first and when he got to the table the first thing he said was, "Good grief, you look just like your brother."

Then he sat down with a thud and stared at me.

"I never realized it before, but with the beard you look just like him."
"What beard?" I enquired.
"OK, so it isn't really a beard, but I have never seen you any way but clean shaven – fastidiously so."

As I absorbed this bells were clanging in my head; I hadn't shaved that morning for some reason, and that explained why my secretary had looked at me that way. This was not good, and certainly was not the impeccable businessman image I wished to portray. I would buy a razor and shave before going back this afternoon, but why hadn't I shaved? I always did, and why had I not noticed when I looked in the mirror?

Not wanting to admit my weird lapse, I made some plausible excuse and we ordered lunch.

"Do you ever think about him?" my school friend asked.

"Now and again, but I try not to as there is nothing I can do about it. No one knows where he is."

"I suppose so. Fair enough", and John changed the subject.

Lunch over, I nipped into a chemist, bought a razor and went into the toilet of a nearby coffee shop to remove the offending item from my face. I still wondered why I hadn't noticed it all morning, but before I got too caught up in that question another problem posed itself. I couldn't shave. There was no real reason why I couldn't do it, but it felt as if someone were pulling my arm down to stop it reaching my face. I tried the other hand but the same thing happened. I tried in vain for as long as I could, but an appointment with my most valued and important client loomed, and I had to leave if I were not going to add tardiness to my day's faults.

After the meeting I found myself sitting, staring into space and thinking, and I could not get my brain back on track to do any work, so, I got my coat and told my secretary to cancel all business for the rest of the day as I was feeling unwell and was going home.

"I did wonder," was all she said as I rushed outside.

I wandered around for a while and soon found myself outside a florist. This was not just any florist; it was where my brother's old fiancée Linda worked. I found myself going in without actually making the decision to do so. Linda's initial reaction was just like John's, looking as if she had seen a ghost, and when I asked if she could take a break and talk, she agreed willingly.

We sat outside in the cold winter's weather nursing two coffees and talked about 'him'. We discussed what Ted had been like, how much fun he had been, but also the dark current that ran underneath and that was seen only by those who got to know him well. Plucking up the courage I told her about the milk and beard.

"It is as if he were trying to make me into him," I added, waiting for some sort of 'you're nuts' exclamation, but instead got, "Yes, I can see how it looks like that – but why?"

"You don't think I am mad then?" I asked, relieved.

"We used to talk about you; he looked up to you even though you were the younger one, but we always said how straight and sensible you were, so knowing how much it must have cost you to make that statement makes me take it very seriously."

Suddenly she remembered she was late getting back to work, and our reminiscences were cut short as she dashed off, with the promise of dinner that evening to continue the talk.

Dinner conversation was all about my brother, or perhaps more accurately, her fiancé. I noticed she still wore her engagement ring, and mention of this brought forth the reply that a part of her still hoped he would turn up for their wedding which should have been on August 9th this year. She said she still loved him, but the hurt he had left her with was so big her head didn't want to feel this. He had walked away without telling her he was going, and, like the rest of us, she had heard nothing more.

The long term forward planning of the wedding had been my doing as they had wanted to get married straight away but had no money and as both still lived at home with their respective parents, nowhere to live. I had suggested they set a date a couple of years hence and start saving for it, using the time to find somewhere to live, and buy items of furniture as and when they could afford it. Linda, being the practical one of the two thought it a good plan, and against my brother's wishes, she, and my whole family, had convinced the out of funds groom to go along with this.

A strange coincidence was that I had taken on the debt my brother had run up when my parents died and hoped to pay the final instalment in August of this year – just when they should have got married.

A few months passed and Linda and I became 'an item', both seeming to enjoy the other's company. We went ice skating, clubbing and spent weekends in Paris, Barcelona and other easily reached destinations – all new pastimes for me and things I had always despised. My brother seemed to have taken over my life, or my life seemed to have become my brother's.

I skipped appointments at work, shaved only occasionally, cleaned my flat less than I used to and started eating those dreadful things called TV dinners. My healthy lifestyle became a health hazard and my meticulous business sense went out the window. Luckily I managed to keep my extremely well paid job just long enough to pay the last of the debt, but no longer. From that first morning everything I did, I did reluctantly, but with no choice. Eventually, in desperation I visited a shrink who suggested my behaviour was due to feelings of guilt about my brother, adding I felt the need to become him to assuage that guilt. I couldn't help thinking that was not right as I had not been involved in his actions either during or after. My parents had discovered the fraud and confronted him before telling me. I saw another psychiatrist who suggested a nervous breakdown, but again I didn't feel this was the answer, or more precisely if I was having a breakdown something had caused it and that was the main problem.

I struggled to understand what was happening to me and talked about it to Linda, who wondered if I felt that in order to win her over I needed to become my brother. I stopped mentioning it to her as the answer, 'It really doesn't matter if I win you over or not, as I am only courting you because I have to', didn't seem appropriate, and was yet another conundrum to unravel.

84

The wedding arrived, which after all was to have been my brother's, but we had left all the arrangements in place, with the simple substitution of my myself as groom instead of my brother. Linda often asked if I thought he would turn up, but I knew beyond any doubt he wouldn't. How I knew this I don't know, and it was another thing to add to the long list of things that needed to be explained, but had no evident answers.

We flew to St. Lucia for our honeymoon, just as they had planned and as I got into our room from an early morning swim on the second day the phone was ringing. I answered and a voice with a French accent asked if I were Ted Morton's brother James. When he ascertained this was correct, he said it wasn't his fault, as Tom Browne had appeared to have no family and if it hadn't been for the photo in the newspaper he wouldn't have known. Seemingly he had spent all day and all night checking and now he knew everything, he informed me – but I didn't have any idea what he was talking about and asked him to explain more clearly.

He did. He had bad news, and had spent months trying to track any relative down. My brother was dead. He had died on 2nd of March at 11.55pm. He had been buried as Tom Browne, which was the name he had been using in Canada, and it was only when a local resident, who had been friends with my brother, had seen my wedding photo in the English newspapers that they managed to discover that this name was an alias, and trace me as his only relative. Apparently they had always wondered if Tom Browne was his real name, as that person seemed not to exist before he landed in Canada, but as he behaved well they didn't bother investigating until now.

I hung up and sat on the bed for a while in shock. Luckily Linda had stayed on the beach for a snooze before it got too hot, so I had some time alone to think. The date had instantly registered as it was the next morning I had started acting like Ted. Now I knew what had happened. Ted was trying to take over my life so he could still do all the things he wanted. Well that was not going to happen. When Linda returned I made an excuse and left the hotel, searching in town for the little place I had seen the day before and once inside explained what I wanted.

Returning to the hotel I washed, shaved and dressed in the smart new business suit I had bought on my way home, before gently explaining to Linda we needed a divorce and why.

Every morning when I wake up the first thing I do is ask myself if I want fresh milk, and only when the answer comes back negative do I get up. That is not freedom.

Rose Crystal

I had become an Italian translator because my grandmother had fallen in love with Pisa during her grand tour. My job choice came about, not for the reasons you might think - family pressure, but a whole other set of circumstances.

My grandfather died when I was twelve and Elise, my grandmother was distraught. My mother thought a good distraction would be to take her mother to Pisa for a break. As luck would have it, my own mother fell from her horse a couple of days before they were due to leave and badly strained a ligament. She had to have total rest for weeks and was even given a wheelchair.

At first grandma was ready to cancel the trip, but then my father hit on the idea of me accompanying her instead. This seemed to solve many problems at once – I was out of the house, making less work, (although I was only told this later in life), my mother had less to worry about and Elise could go to the only place she had no memories of her husband. For some reason Pisa was so special to her she had never gone back after she got married, although she had returned numerous times before that.

I had already travelled with my parents, so had a current passport, and the travel agents my family used were only too happy to change the name from Mrs Hardy to Miss Hardy.

My parents had made my grandmother promise she would make me study in the mornings but, although I envisioned being cooped up indoors all morning, the first time granny and I were alone she said, "All right, we both promised, so it has to be done, but how about this? We get up at 7.00am, like normal, and you study from then until 10.00, after that we go out and see the sights – and we never tell anyone how long you studied?"

I replied that it sounded wonderful and agreed that I would work extra hard during those few hours, (she had threatened that if I didn't, the study period would be extended to lunchtime, which was a strong incentive to concentrate hard on the hated books).

We set off to Italy, and in the end my presence was probably the best thing for grandma as she was kept busy looking after me and had little time to think.

We had a wonderful time and went back together often, and so my love of Italy was born. As I got older I went with friends, and as time wore on I picked up some basic Italian, so it seemed natural to choose that to study when I went to university. It also meant I could realistically go to Italy to look for work, and that excited me. Unlike Elise, my love for that country was not limited to Pisa, and after exploring a few towns, I soon settled on Como, in the north, as the place I wanted to be. It was a wonderful town and forty minutes in the car took me to Lugano, with the great metropolis of Milan just an hour's drive away - and frequent trains ran from Como to Milan as an added bonus.

I found the Italians easy to get along with and had soon made a good group of friends. It was with some of those friends I went to Milan one evening. We intended to walk along the canal and find a place to have a few drinks, before heading off later to go to a disco. When the weather permitted, the canal was lined with artists of all types, from painters and jewellery makers to people who read cards, palms and anything else you offered.

There was a magic atmosphere there that had more to do with the street markets than the psychic aura, and it was a fun night's entertainment; something I had done often, but never with these particular friends.

Maria stopped at the first card reader to ask about her future. She was in love and wanted an answer to the eternal young lady's question, "Is he the one?" The others crowded round to hear everything that was said, but cynical of these things, I hung back expecting the classic and very general, "You will meet a tall, dark, handsome stranger". I was therefore surprised to hear, "You have a man who is no good. He is married but will not tell you. You must stop the relationship before his wife finds out. She will come to see you with their three children and it will be very unpleasant."

She said a few more things, but nothing more of note, I think. Truth to tell I wasn't paying much attention as I was thinking, "Surely these people tell you things you want to hear so you will come back?"

After Maria paid and we were leaving, the lady touched my arm gently and whispered, "You are one of us."

Before I could ask who I was 'one of', she had turned to her next victim and my friends were walking on. The area was packed, as always, and fearful of losing them I rushed to catch up.

Maria was upset. She loved him and he was married! I pointed out that she didn't know for sure yet and would be better advised to find out before getting too upset, as it may not be right.

I don't know whether she believed me or simply made an effort not to ruin the evening for the rest of us, but she did seem to cheer up.

A little further on we stopped at another psychic, medium or whatever you want to call them, as Claudia wanted a reading this time. (Oh no, was it going to one of those evenings where we lurched from one charlatan to another with nothing in between?)

This reading went rather like the first, with Claudia being informed the company she worked for was going to close soon so she needed to start looking for another job. Again, as we were leaving this lady said exactly the same thing to me as the other lady had; the difference was she didn't whisper and the others heard. Laura asked, "Can you read cards too?" and Sara jumped in with, "Why didn't you say?"

"I can't. Was that what she meant?" I inquired.

They assumed so, but I wasn't convinced. About four mediums, of all types, later I did start to have doubts. They had all said the same thing, but one in particular had really made me think. She was a medium, rather than a psychic, (I was learning they were different), and used a crystal on a chain to talk to the spirits. The stone moved in a circle over the correct letter to spell a word, and try as I might I couldn't see her hand move to make the pendulum swing.

She produced another pendulum, (ostensibly it is bad luck for anyone to use hers), and suggested I try, and although I really didn't want to, with everyone egging me on it was easier to just do it. The minute I picked up the crystal it started moving quite strongly. In my mind I went through the various possibilities, such as: I was unconsciously moving it – but that didn't seem to be the case; it was a special crystal that moved for some reason – but as everyone wanted to try and it steadfastly stayed still for the others, this definitely was not the reason. I also thought I might just be seeing it move when it wasn't really, as that was what I expected, but then, being disbelieving about the whole thing, this too didn't hold water as a theory.

Whatever the reason, and I was sure there was a good explanation that did not involve ghosts, I wanted to leave these "Mystic Megs" and look at some of the other stalls and then go to a bar for a drink.

We did leave, but as I had suspected only to go to another "reader" and then another. We visited seven in total, and each one gave some specific information to someone and all of them said the same thing to me, that I was one of them.

By the time we did go for a drink the talk was all about what future had been foretold for everyone, (except me as I had refused to participate), and about my alleged talents and what to do about getting me ready for 'readings'. The fact I kept repeating that I did not believe in that stuff and had no intention of doing any work in that field, seemed to make them more determined, and phrases like, "The fact you don't believe makes it more amazing you can do it and proves it is not a trick," were bandied about a lot.

After the bar we went to a disco and left there in time for breakfast, arriving back in Como about 9.30am. I went to bed for a while and woke at lunchtime - after all it was the weekend. After lunch I started to clean the house but was interrupted by the doorbell.

My friends stood there with a small, beautifully wrapped box and huge grins. I invited them in, put the espresso machine on and opened my gift. It was a beautiful rose quartz crystal pendulum. I admired the crystal while doubting the wisdom of their spending. They wanted me to try it straight away and it seemed petty to refuse after they had taken the trouble to buy me this present, so I did.

The first question was from Maria who wanted to ask if her boyfriend was married. The crystal swung over "yes" and again "yes" when she asked if he had children.

We played for a while and actually I found it great fun, but what worried me was the way the others were taking it so seriously. No matter what the crystal said they were prepared to act on it with no further proof. I counselled caution and at one point felt forced to say I would only continue if they agreed to check things out before acting. Reluctantly they all promised and we discovered that: it would rain that evening, Laura's middle name was Giuseppina, which she hated, Claudia's car needed petrol, (don't ask me why this dilemma was resolved by using the pendulum rather than looking at the dashboard), and many other banal facts. However, my friend's questions like, "should I leave Marco?" or, "should I hand in my notice at work?" continued to plague me, especially as the answer to both was an unequivocal yes. I was still apprehensive that the girls intended to fix their problems without making sure there really was a problem to fix, despite their promise. Their belief in this 'thing' was absolute and seemed to leave no room for reality.

We went to another disco in Milan that evening and one of the questions asked during my session that afternoon came true. One of my friends had asked if I would get picked up, and I did, but as this was always a good bet for any woman in a disco I did not take it as proof. Yes, he was very handsome, as the pendulum had said, but again if he hadn't been, I wouldn't have agreed to dinner on Tuesday evening, (it was a waste of time anyway – he was an idiot, and the crystal hadn't told me that).

Monday was a different story. Maria phoned her new man and asked to see him urgently. She got Laura to be there for backup and from their description of the evening, as soon as he arrived he was questioned about his marital status. It turned out he *was* married but had two children, not three.

My friends insisted this was proof that my psychic abilities did exist, and the "wrong" number of children was due either to him lying, (I couldn't see why he would admit to two children but deny three), or his wife was pregnant and the third did exist, but simply was not born yet.

Claudia's employers were still in business and none of the other prophecies had yet come true, (nor had they been disproved I should add), so they all maintained their faith, and I only used the crystal when they were desperate and I found it hard to refuse.

A few years passed and I learnt that the majority of Italians used some form of clairvoyance to control the direction their lives took. This went from tarot cards and normal cards to reading coffee grains. (Tea was not really drunk in that country, and when it was it was used in bags; coffer grains in the bottom of a cup were the Italian equivalent of tea leaves.)

My friends were never very happy that I didn't believe in this stuff, but they accepted my reluctance and continued to pay so-called experts for "advice", and life continued as normal, with weekdays spent hard at work and weekends going to discos, parties or in winter staying in small hotels in the mountains and skiing.

My grandmother came to stay quite often, and it was a pleasure having her visit. She helped out in the house without, "tidying up by putting things in a better place", which my mother did constantly. Elise also spoke enough Italian to meet my friends and we all went out for ice-creams, walks, shopping and dinner. Neither my parents, nor any other visitors who came to stay, understood any Italian, and my Italian friends spoke no English, which made group events miserable for all involved, and after a few attempts I abandoned the idea.

If any of my friends were free while I was working they often took Elise somewhere, and on one of those occasions the pendulum came up. That evening Elise asked me about it and I explained, embarrassed, but she asked to see it working. In the end she and I sat for hours playing with it and as we both felt the same way, we didn't take it too seriously. Afterwards we did talk about whether or not "playing" with it was a bad idea, but we really didn't think there was anything to it – no one 'up there' making it move, which meant there was nothing or no one to hurt or upset.

Sara's father died one March and her mother became very ill within the space of a few months. The rest of us agreed to take it in turns to stay with her and help with her mother, who refused to go to hospital. I hated going to her house alone, as invariably she wanted me to ask the crystal when her mother would die, and I didn't want to, but it seemed churlish to refuse. I was really worried as she wanted to start organising the funeral on the basis of 'what I said', which was why I didn't want to do it, so we reached a compromise that I would do 'it' any time she wanted as long as she didn't ask that question.

We all knew it would not be long before her mother died too, and so at weekends we cooked meals and took them there so we could all spend the evenings together. One Saturday night, near the end, Sara had just given her mother her midnight medication a few minutes before, and we were talking to my pendulum when I started to feel really strange. It was an odd sensation and one I had never had before, sort of fear, (although abject terror would be closer), a knot in my stomach, shakes – but inside not on the outside. I didn't know what it was and was in the process of thinking it might be some sort of strange flu when the crystal flew straight out to the side and taking me unaware hovered horizontally over my phone which was sitting on the table.

Now, the chain was thin and was just like a necklace chain – flexible and soft – so there was no way, in theory, that the crystal could sit out at a right-angle, but it did. I looked up and everyone had blanched.

It then went to the alphabet we had written on a piece of paper and spelt out, "I am gone, my dear". That was odd as we had always conducted these sessions in Italian. My friends asked what it had said, but I didn't want to say anything as Sara would immediately believe her mother had died, so instead, played for time, I suggested someone should check on Signora Mordelli as we hadn't done so for a while. Luckily Sara went, (not remembering she had been with her mother not long before), so I quickly told the others what had been spelt out. We sat in silence until Sara returned to tell us her mother was fine but would like a drink of water.

I used the time it took Sara to take the drink in, to ask the crystal who was speaking, but instead of answering it started to pull strongly on the chain, so much so I had trouble keeping it in my grasp, and finally I followed it until it came to rest on top of my phone. No sooner had it done this than my phone rang. I knew it was late, but was not sure how late, so I glanced at my watch before answering. It was 12.32am.

I picked up the phone and a voice in English told me my grandmother had died at three minutes past midnight. Right at the time I had started to feel fear. Now I knew beyond any doubt - and I often spoke to Elise after that.

The Wine Cellar

I had married above me, everyone said so, and to be truthful I knew it without anyone having to point it out. My wife Caroline and my mother-in-law didn't seem to have any difficulty with my 'lowness', but my father-in-law Alistair, was a different story. He lost no opportunity to remind everyone, and I do mean everyone, that I was beneath his family. At parties he made comments such as, "This is a very nice sherry – of course my daughter's friend wouldn't know because he was born to the class that thinks cooking sherry is the height of decadence". He couldn't bring himself to admit I had actually married his daughter, and to his death I remained nameless, as 'James' seemed to choke him. In private the comments were less guarded, and after offering me a huge sum to get a quick divorce, which I refused, as I really loved Caroline, he decided the only way to get rid of me was to make my life as difficult as possible in the hope I would leave.

When Georgina, Caroline's mother, died, Alistair got worse as she had curtailed his antics whenever possible, and I do think the hatred for me, that he let boil inside him, attributed to his heart attack. In my saner moments I knew it really wasn't personal and he would have hated anyone who married his prized possession. My lack of breeding was just an excuse, and if the problem hadn't been that you can be sure there would have been something else. Whatever the cause of his illness, he was no longer capable of living alone, and as the family 'pile', (as he lovingly called the huge mansion that had been in his family since the beginning of time), was entailed and would pass to his only child, Caroline, we had little choice but to move in with him.

Not once did it enter his head that to do this I had had to give up my good job in corporate law, (which I had really enjoyed), leave behind my own home and move to live sixty miles from my friends and my own family. I suppose a part of me had, unrealistically, hoped he would appreciate my sacrifice and change his ways, but I should have known better.

Alistair was born noble, rich and just plain bad. He also was rather devious and seldom said or did anything untoward in front of his daughter. The only thing that kept me there were his daughter's words on those rare occasions when he slipped up with her present. Hearing unpleasant remarks about me, she threatened to leave if he couldn't treat me better. It didn't occur to him, and no amount of pointing it out helped, that by hurting me he was also hurting his precious Caroline.

I ran the estate while Caroline ran the house and servants, as well as her father. That suited us all, because most days I was out of the house or in the room I had made my office, and we only met for dinner. Alistair tired easily and usually went to bed straight after the meal, leaving us free to enjoy the evening. We had an unspoken rule about not talking about her father then, so these times were pleasurable. He was the only blot on an otherwise idyllic marriage and we were still as much in love as when we had met.

Alistair had many ways of going about obtaining a divorce and provoking me was only one. Another idea was to show me up in front of Caroline, (so she would leave me), and he hit upon a way guaranteed to do just that.

'His type', as he was fond of saying, knew which wine went with which food and felt the meal was ruined if an incorrect wine were served. With this in mind, he used his decreased mobility as an excuse to ask me to go to their immense wine cellar every evening to select wine for dinner. He was convinced I would choose badly and look inadequate in Caroline's eyes, and I must say I tended to agree with him, (while I silently cursed his ill health that afforded him time to think up new tortures for me).

He suggested I 'liaise' with Caroline so I would know what we were eating. I had every intention of liaising with Caro, but not in the way he intended, and besides, even knowing what we were to eat told me nothing about which wine to choose. I wasn't a philistine and could recognise good wine, but one that went well with chicken seemed to me to suit turkey just as well. The problem was he didn't share my sentiment, and Caroline also preferred something different for these two fowl dishes. The first time I asked her about dinner she told me we were having Beef Bourguignon, kindly adding, "I love a good Cabernet Sauvignon with it as it is high in tannins and counters the rich beef stew so well".

A hint, aimed at helping, but finding a bottle among thousands that said Cabernet Sauvignon would be no mean feat. I knew it was red, so could rule out the whites, but it still was a daunting task.

Normally I had developed a thick skin for Alistair's Machiavellian tricks, but for some reason choosing the right wine seemed important to me.

Feeling like the chatelaine of the castle I took out my bunch of keys and descended into the depths that were the wine cellar with a good degree of trepidation.

The room contained white, red and fizzy wine by the ton, along with a few special bottles of brandy, whisky and other odd bottles collected over generations, and my particular favourite was a bottle of white Campari. I had tried looking for this on the internet, but the company seemed to have stopped making it sometime around 1940, and even then they only seemed to have made a few bottles. I loved Campari, and had my father-in-law been different, I might have suggested opening it, but - as it was, I worshipped this unique bottle from afar. Also in the open space just inside the door was a table, a corkscrew, glasses and decanters so you could choose a bottle, open it and taste it, to be sure it was not corked, before decanting it ready for use. I would taste the bottle I picked that evening, but with my fingers crossed, for unless it was really bad, I probably couldn't tell the difference.

When I switched on the light, what I immediately noticed was an open bottle sitting on the table beside a glass with a small amount already poured. My first thought was that my father-in-law had tried to trick me by deliberately tempting me to choose the wrong bottle, but upon reflection I reasoned he could not negotiate the steps to get here. Maybe one of the staff had done it at his bidding, but even that seemed unlikely. The servants didn't like Alistair and all loved Caroline, so by association I was acceptable. (My parents were not lower class and I had grown up with a nanny, housemaids and gardener, so knew how to behave with them, which helped.) I wondered if they would help Alistair when it would hurt Caroline, and thought it unlikely, but not totally out of the question.

After much thought I tried to play it safe, and finding a Cabernet Sauvignon, opened it, tasting both my choice and the already open bottle, and finding them extremely palatable I took both to Caro saying, "I was unsure which was best, which do you prefer?"

She chose the one that had already been opened and at the table I watched her father's disappointment as he too found it suitable.

Relief at having 'got it right' vied with curiosity as to who had pointed me in the right direction. I finally decided 'the butler did it', trite as that might sound, as he was the only one who might have enough knowledge, but if it was him he obviously did not want me to know, otherwise he would have 'suggested' a wine, rather than sneaking down and opening it for me.

The next evening I went down the steps wondering, and hoping, that my saviour would have another bottle ready for me. He did, or she did. Suddenly I wondered if it was Caro doing it, and not wanting to show me up she was doing it in secret. The butler was fine, but Caroline wasn't. I would have preferred she teach me how to know which wine suited what food, rather than this subterfuge, so resolved to find out.

That second evening I hit the nail on the head again, or judging by my father-in-law's dour expression, the nail seemed to be in his coffin.

This ritual persisted for quite a few nights and I gave up looking for a bottle, simple settling for the one poured – it was always 'perfect', so why bother. I did however try to establish who it could be, but had to rule out Caro when we got back late from a day out, and going straight to the cellar I found the habitual bottle ready for me. She had been with me all day and could not have laid the bottle out. I did try an obscure conversation about wine with Jones, the butler, but he gave away nothing and I did not want to push too much for fear the help I was getting would stop.

Not happy with my continued success Alistair tried a new tack. One day he said he wanted a specific bottle to have with dinner that evening. Time had taught me that easy living meant going along with his wishes without raising an eyebrow or asking any questions, so I would provide the bottle he wished, but again it was sitting on the table ready for me. Now that did make me think a bit more - who could have known he would request, (actually demand), that specific wine?

I had become used to second guessing Alistair, but on this occasion I couldn't figure out what the catch was, and that worried me, although I had no doubt there was one somewhere in the mix. When he made an excuse for not drinking wine during the meal that evening I became really suspicious, but of what I still didn't know. When he produced a 'special' bottle of wine for Caroline only, I became paranoid and thought he might have poisoned the wine. Unfortunately I had already consumed enough for any damage to be already done, so it would be too late if that were the case, but I felt fine and perfectly normal. After that I drank only water, just in case – you never know.

The next evening he asked for the same wine and again claimed ill health prevented him from imbibing. Again Caro had a gift bottle all to herself, but this time I only pretended to drink. I noticed Alastair watched me attentively and as I sat playing with my food, (I had lost my appetite), I wondered about getting my blood red glass of liquid tested for poison, although I did feel a bit foolish even thinking it.

The following evening was a repeat; except my wife declined the bottle produced for her and poured a generous dose from the decanter. I noted the panic flit over Alistair's face. Something was wrong and it wasn't paranoia making me think it, but I didn't know what was going on. It was all very well thinking he had poisoned the wine, but I really didn't think he would murder me, much as he would love someone to do it.

For about five nights in a row the same charade continued, until one night he didn't make any excuses and prepared to drink it with us. He raised a toast to Caroline and took a healthy swallow. We followed suit, but before we got our glasses to our lips they shattered. About the same time the wine decanter also broke and as we were cleaning up the wine spilt all over the table, Alastair made an odd noise and died.

The doctor came and pronounced Alastair's heart had given up, and we took a distraught Caroline upstairs where the doctor gave her a mild sedative. She was very upset, but I think part of the problem was knowing her family had all gone now and she was alone, although she had been very fond of the old so and so too. When she was asleep I went downstairs and with Jones' help organised the family undertaker and others to come and do the necessary things.

Jones suggested a glass of brandy and mentioned a good one in the cellar he thought I would enjoy. He offered to get it for me, (proving he did have the keys and therefore could have helped me out with the wine), but I felt the need to go there myself and this provided the perfect excuse. I loved the room and its feel of ancient times with all their stories, and my only aid had come from there, so it seemed right my solace should too. I was sad, not about Alastair's parting, but that he had not let me into the family and had made things so difficult. I was sad for what could have been, and to be honest somewhat relieved Alastair would no longer hound us all.

I opened the door to find the bottle of white Campari open and poured into a glass, and myself in the middle of a conversation between two people. One was Georgina and the other a male voice a bit like Alastair's.

"I don't think he will be joining us here", said the man.

Georgina replied, "No, somehow I doubt it, but poor James doesn't understand it all and looks baffled".

She was wrong there, well she was right about my not understanding, but baffled was an understatement.

"Let me explain", said the man and proceeded to do so.

"I am Sebastian, Alastair's father. I died young because my own son poisoned my wine so he could get his hands on my money and social position as owner of this estate. At the time I didn't know it, but I did learn what happened later. He took half a dozen bottles of that wine you have been drinking for the last lot of days and injected various levels of poison through the corks.

Alistair pretended an infection and invented anti-biotic pills he had to take that precluded him drinking alcohol, so while I consumed poison he drank water and I thought nothing of it. He gave me one with little poison at first to make sure I did not taste anything odd and built up the dose each night until finally I drank a bottle filled with enough poison to kill an elephant. But that was in bottle number five, and there was one bottle left with even more poison in it. He had placed the six toxic bottles in the top row, on the right, leaving one space between them and the healthy wine of the same label.

When my son suggested you choose the wine I worried you might pick up that bottle and all three of you drink it, so I set out a bottle for every night. Also, both Georgina and I like you and believe you make Caroline happy, so it was a pleasure to thwart Alistair and help you select the correct wine.

Having tried, and failed, at getting you to leave by yourself, Alistair remembered the last remaining lethal bottle and felt he had no alternative but to get you to drink it.

At first I simply set out the bottles with no poison in them, but eventually we were down to the last bottle and I had no choice. I had thought of breaking the bottle, but Georgina suggested the time had come to let you two young people enjoy life, so I set out the poisoned bottle already decanted, hoping you would not taste it, but I was ready in case you did. Georgina and I waited in the dining room to make sure you and Caroline didn't drink any of that wine, and it was us who broke your glasses and the decanter. We had discussed it and knew Alistair might drink some, believing he had miscalculated and had in fact used up all the poisoned bottles all those years ago, but we also chose to do nothing about it. The effects of this lethal vintage look like a heart attack and, as I too died of a supposed heart attack while young, it will be supposed it is a family trait."

"Now we must leave you", Georgina said. "You can do with this knowledge whatever you feel best. If you get the tablecloth analysed it will show up the poison, otherwise everything can be left as natural causes."

Unsure what to do, I made sure the tablecloth did not get washed until I had had time to make up my mind. Caroline made it up for me the next day by saying, "Daddy was behaving oddly about the wine the last few days, asking for the same wine and not drinking it, then giving me a different one. At one time I did wonder if he was trying to poison you, and don't look so shocked. I did know how miserable he made your life, but short of trying to love you more I didn't see what I could do about it."

It was the next question that settled it in my mind.

"Do you think he had tried to kill you and having failed, committed suicide?"

"Caro, we didn't drink because our glasses broke, and he couldn't have foreseen that."

"No, but …. Oh, it is just awful not knowing what happened. I just know there is more to it, but can't figure out what."

"Sit down and I will tell you", I suggested.

I had worried she would be even more upset, but instead she seemed to relax and be more at peace.

"I kept dreaming of Mummy who visited me and said, "Be careful. He did it to me so he could have you to himself."

I hadn't thought of that, but "Your mother died of a heart attack at an early age, didn't she?"

"Yes. Oh................"

Thief of Hearts

"Stand and deliver! Your money or your life! If no one does anything heroic, nobody will be hurt."

No one did and I relieved them of their worldly goods, or at least as many as they had with them, before riding off to the inn where I lived. After stabling Tory I went in through the back door, and in the safety of my room I looked to see what the night's work had provided. The result was a good enough haul under normal circumstances, but I wanted more than the prize on the bed to give to Sally.

Sally owned half of the inn, but the other half was a problem. Her husband Tom, who had been my best friend and partner in crime, (literally), had died a few months ago without a will, and the law decreed half the inn went to Sally and the other half to Tom's stuffy brother John. He hadn't intended leaving any to the silly idiot, but by diving into icy water to save a child and dying intestate, that is what happened. Now John was trying to sell the place and I wanted to save it for Sally's sake.

Sally and Tom had taken me in when I was desperate and it had been my home for a few years, and was Sally's only means of income. I had already got nearly half the money to buy out the greedy brother, but time was running out to find the rest, and John had already stated he would not wait. If we had not bought out his share within twenty one days, the inn would be sold at public auction.

I had some jewellery to sell, but absolutely no idea of its value. That had been one of the things Tom had taken care of, disappearing for a few days with a bag full of baubles and returning mysteriously with a wad of cash.

Three weeks might seem long enough to gather together the money, but the problem was I couldn't risk going out onto the road every night. The authorities tended to post watchers the day after a robbery and leave them in place for a few days, so I had to let some time elapse before doing it again in relative safety. That left me three or four more possible robberies and I just had to hope enough carriages passed and that each carried a good supply of money.

Oh well, off to bed and then tomorrow I would do odd jobs around the inn to help Sally, and tomorrow night a bit of service behind the bar. Tom and I had found that, by being seen to work, customers remembered seeing us, but few would be sure which night, (they all tended to drink rather a lot and got confused).

Being extra cautious was why Tom and I had been so successful and managed to stay ahead of the law for so long.

Life was normal for a few days and then one day Sally overheard some talk about a carriage of silly rich folk carrying a big bag of cash and travelling north that evening. It sounded too good to miss, so I got ready for business.

Everything went as planned, until everyone got out of the carriage. The most beautiful girl I had ever seen stood in front of me. It was not just her looks, there was more to it than that - I felt as if I knew her already and had done for a long time. Unfortunately in these circumstances I couldn't do much about it. Holding someone at gun point to rob them was not good way to make friends, so I put the young lady out of my mind and did what I had come for without incident.

This time I had got a lot of jewellery as well as a bag full of money and I knew the time had come to either find Tom's buyer or get another. Tom had often said the buyer was "one of my lot", and I had always assumed he meant noblemen - but I couldn't just walk up to a likely candidate and ask if they bought stolen goods. I reflected sadly that the time had come for Lord Devonshire to return from 'abroad', so I took my best clothes from my bag, hoping they would fit and prepared to leave.

The thought of returning to civilisation had occupied my thoughts so much I had neglected to empty the bag of money. I remedied this by turning the contents onto the bed, where, amongst the loot was a book. Surprised, I opened to see why it was important enough to be kept with other valuables. I soon realised why and couldn't wait to read it. It would have to go to London with me though, as having made up my mind I had a stagecoach to catch.

I gathered together all the money and gave it to Sally before departing, making her promise to look after Tory while I was away. I couldn't risk taking my horse with me as I was supposed to have just returned from abroad and would have to explain where I had got a horse from.

The coach left at noon the next day and I was on it. I spent the journey reflecting on the welcome I would receive at home - or rather the scenes that awaited me. When my elder brother Edward inherited the earldom he had also inherited the obligation to feed, clothe and house me, but nothing could make the miserable skunk happy about it, and that was why I had taken to the road in the first place.

He treated the estate workers abominably, and when one of our oldest and most loyal employees had needed an advance on his salary, to save his child's life, I had robbed my first man in order to get that money. The father had received an anonymous packet with the cash and quickly put it to its intended use. The child had been saved, which felt great, and truth to tell I had enjoyed the escapade. Perhaps the fact I had robbed the very same brother who had refused the loan was part of the satisfaction, but that was when I decided where my future lay. Now I was going back to the dark atmosphere in his home - no, our home, as, whether he liked it or not it was my home too.

Arriving there the servants gave me a warm welcome and good news - my brother was in the country with a party of friends and wouldn't be back until the end of the week.

After I had changed into some of the clothes I had left behind, I thought a ride might help cheer me up and headed to the stables. I was astonished to see Joseph, the man whose daughter had been ill. He too was surprised to see me and the first words out of his mouth shocked me more. "Bless you your Lordship. She is doing well".

Recovering quickly I tried to pretend ignorance, but he quickly put my mind at rest saying, "Who do you think Tom gave the stuff to? I knew straightaway it was you sent the money, and when you left I knew where you had gone, so I asked to be transferred to London. My uncle makes jewellery and I wanted to cut down the risk of you being caught, so I contacted Tom, swearing him to secrecy."

At least that was my problem resolved easily, so I told him that was the only reason I had come back. We arranged the exchange but I would have to wait for his uncle to evaluate the stuff before paying, and that would take a day or two. It would be great if I could get away before the Earl's return, but in the meantime I needed to go out into that vacuous place called society to quell any rumours about my presence.

I had a meal and left reluctantly with an invitation addressed to my brother. I disliked these gatherings, but there would be enough talk about my return without people wondering why I was hiding at home.

I was late arriving and the place was full, but I spotted the young lady from the carriage immediately. Unfortunately a "matchmaking mother" recognised me just as quickly and brought her daughter over to meet the eligible bachelor. (If only she knew!) I put up with the mother and daughter pair for a while as they were able to introduce me to newcomers who had entered the social set in the years during my absence, and there was one particular newcomer I was keen to meet.

I finally got the introduction and Sabrina was as charming as I could have wished for. She was fresh, spontaneous and honest and she admitted her mother insisted she attend these functions to find a titled husband. I was tempted to enquire if a lord would do, but by her mother's indifference to me, I already knew the answer.

Further information taught me she had grown up neither poor nor rich, then, a few years ago a small investment her father had made turned into an extremely profitable earner. He had invested more in other unknown, but subsequently successful enterprises, making him very rich indeed. I had liked him instantly and hoped to have the chance of getting to know him better - for more than one reason.

Sabrina let slip she was going to another party the following night because her mother had decided some earl or other was to be her husband and as he was not here tonight, her mother hoped to find him at the party tomorrow evening . Her father didn't like him and Sabrina hated him, but he was the King's cousin and therefore perfect. Alarm bells were ringing loudly so I tested them on the matchmaking mother.

"I believe you know my brother, the Earl of Devonshire?"

That connection made me suddenly very popular and I was even invited to their home for tea the next day. I accepted, saying to her father I hoped he would be there. I could see that my brother's name had gained points with the matriarch, but I had lost an equal number with her husband, and this made me feel warmer towards the poor downtrodden man.

Seeing the girl from the carriage had reminded me of the mysterious book forgotten in my travelling bag, and when the evening drew to a close I went home and started it.

Over the next few days I learnt everything there was to know about Sabrina: her favourite food, what she enjoyed and what she hated, how she felt about her wonderful father and despicable mother. She was constantly surprised when I expressed an opinion and it perfectly matched hers. I knew her dreams and fears, and for the first time, I wondered about the morality of what I was doing.

I read in the book, "Women hate insincere flattery and would rather be told some of their hair had escaped the arrangement", and said to Sabrina, "I hope you will believe me when I say this is only to help you, but perhaps you might wish to pin your hair up a little tighter." She thanked me warmly and did so.

When I read, "A good gift for a woman would be something they could keep and enjoy every day as a memory, not ostentatious objects to be shown off for the benefit of others", I sent a rose bush to her home.

I thought she was starting to care for me, although as long as I was a highway man I could not do anything about keeping her in my life, but then again I couldn't let her marry my odious brother who I knew was marrying the money and not the woman. (Our country estate and large townhouse cost a lot to keep looking good, and appearances were everything to Edward, Earl of Devonshire.)

Before doing anything about Sabrina I needed to sort Sally out, so with regret, when I received a large sum for the jewels, I told Sabrina I had to go abroad for a while but I would be back. She told me she would wait for me if I wished. That clinched it, and I decided there and then that I would stop roaming the roads and find a job, but first I had to be a bit honest, (although not too much so); "You don't know me and there are things you may not like", I informed her.

"I do know you and I don't care."

It sounded so simple and maybe it was, but conscience dictated another try.

"What if you discovered I was a criminal?" I tried.

"I would assume you had good reason and would protect you."

So it was that simple.

I went to see Sam, her father, the next day before leaving, and told him I had to go abroad as I had promised to help a friend in need, but when I came back I intended to get a job and once settled would like permission to marry his only daughter.

I had expected protestations but he surprised me by saying he had always thought his son-in-law would take over his business, but that he had no intention of having my brother anywhere near him, so whatever happened, if I wanted it, there was a job with him. He even went as far as saying he would keep his wife's matrimonial plans in check until I returned, but winning Sabrina over was up to me. I told him I thought that was more than fair and bid the family farewell.

Sally was pleased to see me. She and I had been like brother and sister since the day we met, so it gave me enormous pleasure to hand over the bounty from the jewellery. This brought the total up to almost enough, but with only two days left I needed one last haul, so although tired after the journey back, I changed and set off straight away.

Luck was with me, as a lone rider came past the trees where I was hiding not long after I got there, and he had a large bag of gold coins. I checked the amount before heading home in case I needed to wait for another victim, but he had enough money to take me over the total. (He was a tax collector so I felt no guilt, knowing how he forced poor people to part with their money.) There was no point taking any risks I didn't need to, so having completed what I needed to do, I went back, relieved it was over.

Sally took the money joyfully, insisting half the inn was mine and there would be a monthly income waiting for me. She made me a meal and we talked long into the night. I told her about Sabrina and about the book. She thought Sabrina and her father sounded lovely, but pointed out the horrendous mother was part of the package. She also expressed doubts about me lasting in a proper job. These were the same doubts I had, but if that were the price for having Sabrina by my side, so be it.

I waited until everything with the inn was finalised and John had been paid off, and sadly prepared to leave.

The next day Sally wished me well and said we should not meet again once I left as it would be too dangerous, adding she would send my earnings from the inn to whatever address I sent her. I did not agree, and felt that if we were careful and told part of the truth - that she was my friend's widow, it would not arouse suspicion, but ever practical she pointed out she was not of my class and that was suspicious enough. We did not resolve this, and would have to wait to see what the future held.

This time my precious Tory was coming with me. I had chosen her because she had no markings, and as there would be no more midnight jaunts, there seemed to be no risk.

Before saying goodbye, Sally told me to burn the book, and seeing an obstinate look cross my face, sat me down for a serious talk. She pointed out that as a woman she knew how women felt about that sort of thing, and I had few alternatives, none pleasant, unless I burnt it. Apparently if I confessed to Sabrina that I had read her diary so I could get to know her better, not only would I be admitting I was a highwayman, but it would cast a huge cloud of doubt on everything I had said. She would never know what had been real and what was based on her most intimate outpourings, which should have remained secret. If I

106

didn't confess, living together and keeping it hidden for ever would not be easy and was a risk.

I didn't destroy it, but it stayed well hidden.

I lived with my brother until the wedding, and that was actually fun because he was so mad at me for stealing his bride, (she had never been that no matter what he thought), he refused to speak to me, so I lived in relative peace.

Work with Sam, was actually fun, and as his daughter's happiness was his foremost concern, I got days off for picnics, Ascot, Henley and anything else I wanted. In return, I used my connections to drum up some good business, and even managed to get Sam into a small gentleman's club which delighted him. All this business involved entertaining, and that kept the mother at bay a bit, and when her husband pointed out that I was also the king's cousin, she came to tolerate me.

One year of marriage and everything was perfect. To celebrate I had got my head stableman's uncle to make a special necklace, (naturally as soon as my father-in-law gave us a house as a wedding present, I had asked Joseph to work for me). Sabrina loved it and said she would put it in her 'special drawer' along with the diary she had started the minute we were engaged. She opened the drawer, and setting the box inside, removed a book with the same cover as the one I had found in the bag. She handed it to me saying, "This is my diary and I want you to read the first entry as I am tired pretending".

Cautiously I turned a page and read, "He thinks I don't know, but I knew the minute he spoke. I wish he trusted me enough to say something but Daddy says he could never take that risk."

"Does your mother know too?" I asked with my mind racing.

"Don't be silly, she would never understand, but when I told Daddy he said you must love me a lot to give it up."

I told her I loved her and thought she was very understanding and then told her about Tom and Sally. She insisted we visit Sally that weekend and it was only the first of many.

Printed in Great Britain
by Amazon